## By the Same Author

*Fax Me a Bagel*

# NEVER NOSH A MATZO BALL

A Ruby, the Rabbi's Wife Mystery

Sharon Kahn 1934-

Scribner

New York London Sydney Singapore

SCRIBNER
1230 Avenue of the Americas
New York, NY 10020

This book is a work of fiction. Names, characters, places, and incidents either are products of the author's imagination or are used fictitiously. Any resemblance to actual events or locales or persons, living or dead, is entirely coincidental.



Designed by Brooke Koven
Text set in Perpetua
Manufactured in the United States of America

1 3 5 7 9 10 8 6 4 2

Library of Congress Cataloging-in-Publication Data
Kahn, Sharon, 1934–
Never nosh a matzo ball: a Ruby, the rabbi's wife mystery/Sharon Kahn.
p. cm.
I. Title.
PS3561.A397N48 2000
813'.54—dc11 99-41311
CIP

ISBN 0-684-84738-8

*For Emma and Camille, with all my love.*

*May your lives unfold exactly as you plan.*
*And if not—*
*just get your bearings and take a different turn.*
*It works.*

# Acknowledgments

To my family: David, Suzy, Jon, and Nancy, for their loving support and for laughing in all the right places.

To those who've helped in so many ways: Ruthe Winegarten, Suzanne and Ned Bloomfield, Lindsy Van Gelder, Pamela Brandt, Nancy Bell, Kathi Stein, Chris Neil, Deena Mersky, Nancy Hendrickson, and Charlene Crilley.

To the Shoal Creek Writers: Judith Austin Mills, Karen Casey Fitzjerrell, Dena Garcia, and Eileen Joyce—you keep me going.

Enduring appreciation to my mainstays: Helen Rees of the Helen Rees Agency, and Susanne Kirk—vice president and executive editor of Scribner. Thanks to Joan Mazmanian, Bill Contardi of the William Morris Agency, and all those at Scribner who helped guide this book along its way.

Special thanks to those who added pleasure and personal touches to long days of book tour travel: Mabel Becker, Charlotte Fox, Joan Weinberg, Sue Elwell, Nurit Shein, Pauline Gilbert, Priscilla Leith, Harriet Pemstein, Linda Nadell, Ruth Dickstein, Eve Schocket, and Nikki Chayet. I enjoyed the hospitality of the Jewish book fairs and the warmth and welcome of so many booksellers.

Last, but not least, thanks to Anne George for her enthusiasm and for wanting a wedding in Ruby's next book!

# NEVER NOSH
# A
# MATZO BALL

# 1

I always wondered if exercise could kill you, and now I'm about to find out.

"Kevin, you're drifting."

He's too busy doing the water aerobics version of cross-country skiing to hear me, so I yell it.

"*You're drifting!*"

Too late. Kevin's short, hairy, and hefty frame is inexorably backing into me as he treads through the water on pretend skis, and he knocks me like an eight ball, right into Essie Sue's line just behind me. She delivers a swift, defensive kick. Why didn't I think of that?

We've now caused a three-line pileup, throwing the

water aerobics class into an uproar. Celeste, our teacher—a cute brunette and ninety-nine-pound role model—is forced to run over and turn off the accompaniment tape of *Rock with the Classics*. Trust me, she'd rather eat solid cholesterol than interrupt the High Intensity portion of our daily workout. I say "daily" with a grain of kosher salt, since three days a week is all I can take of being sandwiched between my old nemesis, Essie Sue Margolis, and our new spiritual leader at Temple Rita, Rabbi Kevin Kapstein.

"Rabbi and Ruby, why can't you stay in your lines like everyone else?" Just as I thought, this is Celeste's vision of the apocalypse.

"I didn't do anything. He bumped into me." Even in school, I hated it when they lumped you all together without finding out who was at fault.

Celeste isn't hearing any of it. She's looking out for her boss. "Are you all right, Mrs. Margolis?" I'm *Ruby*—Essie Sue is *Mrs. Margolis,* I notice. Of course, I'm not the new half-owner of the Center for Bodily Movement, either. If I were, you can bet the gym's name wouldn't sound like something you need extra plumbing for.

Essie Sue insisted she wanted the name to reflect the "dignified spirit" of her new venture—"gym" sounded much too sweaty. Not that she wanted to keep males away—her first gesture was to present Kevin with an honorary membership. "It's smart business," she said, and who am I to second-guess? It remains to be seen if he'll have the male population of Eternal flocking after him. So far, the composition of our particular class is fifteen women and two men—the other man is Mr. Chernoff. He drives Mrs. Chernoff and stays.

"You're a menace, Ruby!" Essie Sue concentrates on me. "I think I broke a toenail."

She lifts a tanned leg, waxed smooth enough to make a plucked Empire chicken jealous. "See? My pedicurist waited two weeks for a bottle of Bronze Goddess polish to come in, and now a whole corner of the nail is torn."

I'm still reeling over the fact that she has a pedicurist. I only know from manicurists. When I had my first and only manicure, I was expecting the dominatrix type I'd observed in the hair salon—the one who grabbed your hand and shoved it unbidden from bowl to bowl. Unfortunately, my young lady had just graduated from beauty school, and our encounter was something like two virgins having sex. She expected me to know where to dip, and I was waiting daintily to be dunked. We never quite got the do-si-do right, and I didn't have the patience to go look for a better handshake. The story of my life.

Twelve other class members are now shivering chest-deep in cold water, and I know Celeste won't interrupt Essie Sue, so I do.

"I'll spring for a new pedicure, Essie Sue, but only when Kevin pays for my medical bills—he left bruises all over my body when he slammed into me. Let's get back to the exercise."

Celeste looks extremely disappointed—in me, of course. The others seem to have gotten off unscathed. "We've lost all our momentum," she says, glaring at me, "and I don't know what to do about it. I'm supposed to keep you in the high breathing range for twenty minutes, with ten minutes for cooldown. But we only have fifteen minutes left before the next class."

Uh-oh. She's panicking. Don't look at me. I couldn't solve those eighth-grade math problems about the train ten miles from the next station at seventy-three miles an hour with an unexpected stop, so don't expect me to solve this.

I don't have to. "Put on the *William Tell* Overture," Essie Sue barks, "and get us into double time. I'm not letting Ruby Rothman spoil my workout—I'm under orders from my personal trainer."

*Oy*. Her personal trainer, yet. Another one of her money-saving ideas. If this guy is a personal trainer, I'll eat my weight in matzo balls. Bogie, as he so charmingly calls himself, is a wanna-be tough guy whose persona comes across more like Clark Kent on acid. Essie Sue hired him because he claimed to be Mr. Texas Muscle and also because he accepted her salary range. I have no doubt which qualification pushed him over the top. Now I'm involved with him because The Hot Bagel, my own new venture in entrepreneurship, is a sponsor of the All Faiths Baseball Team. Essie Sue loaned out Bogie as the coach and, in a giant leap of faith, just appointed our own Rabbi Kevin Kapstein to play for the Temple. She says it'll enhance the Temple's image. I can't wait to e-mail this latest sports bulletin to my friend Nan in Seattle. She saved my life long-distance last year when we had a killer in the bakery, and she knows all about the Terrible Twosome, Kevin and Essie Sue.

Celeste jumps out of the water to put on *William Tell*. She's smiling. Now it's her boss's responsibility if we all drop dead. I don't think you're supposed to go from standing in the water to double time, but what do I know?

No more with the cross-country ski. We do a fast jog in a circle, wall to wall. Those who can't keep up get trampled on unless they're quick enough to move aside, which, being the slow ones, they usually aren't. The rules of the road don't apply here, unless you happen to be driving in Rome. Essie Sue's headed right for me, but I run faster than she does.

"Reverse!" This is the special torture Celeste saves for the moment the current has built up in one direction, allowing slackers to go with the flow.

Ha! Essie Sue is having trouble reversing, and she sneakily grabs on to Kevin's arm underwater as ballast.

"You're cheating," I say sweetly as I charge past them.

Our circle is now looking more like ring-around-the-rosy than the Charge of the Light Brigade. Mr. Chernoff has dropped to his knees, causing Celeste to do a quick body count. I sympathize with her, though—you don't buck Essie Sue so easily. Not in this life.

I'm here because I'm cheap. When Essie Sue bought the place a few months ago, she offered Founding Member discounts—not that we're founding members of anything. Essie Sue wanted a classy tone for the spa, as she now calls the former Sam's Gym, our little town of Eternal's only prior attempt at fitness. Fitness was not what Sam originally had in mind, I should point out. He managed wrestlers at the time, and the gym was a hangout for his buddies. He went bankrupt when he overextended himself by putting in a pool. He should have put in a pool *table,* but he found that out too late.

It's a leap from Sam's to classy, trust me, but I love the water and the exercise is great—I alternate the water aerobics classes with lap swimming on my own time. Other than making the half hour trip up to Austin where fitness centers abound, this my best choice—I can fall out of bed early in the morning and be ready for the rest of my day by nine o'clock. I can use all the time I can get. Today I have to order supplies and check on the help at the bakery (my partner Milt's handling the lunch rush), then put on my other hat as a computer consultant. Leffert Jewelers' newly installed accounting software is telling them they have six million dollars on hand. I don't think so.

We're finished with circles and are now jogging backward. "This is very good for your gluteus maximus," Celeste yells, patting her own behind. Kevin, displaying more maximus than Celeste recommends, is, as usual, not looking behind him as he jogs. Before Celeste can get to the rectus abdominis, one of her very favorite body parts that sounds so horrendous I can never remember what it actually represents, Kevin smashes into—not me, thank heavens, but Essie Sue, who's completely knocked off her long, slender pins and flung under the water. Head-first.

Uh-oh—he's committed the one unpardonable sin. You'd think anyone joining a water aerobics class might expect to be exposed to moisture once in a while, but not in this case. Essie Sue does not intend to have her Golden Honey sculpted cut to be altered by the elements—ever. He's in for it now.

She rises from the deep with the wrath of a Rhine maiden, minus the avoirdupois, and heads straight for me.

"If you were in your rightful place behind him, this would never have happened, Ruby."

Some things never change.

# 2

E-mail from: Ruby
To: Nan
Subject: *We Dropped the Ball*

How's the course in Contracts going? I know you're overwhelmed with the first year of law school—in fact, I'm amazed you still find time to write me back. Of course, babe, in a life now consisting solely of study and work, yakking with me must be positively liberating—ha. On my end, I'll try to keep up the diversions for you, and trust me, there's no shortage.

She's done it again. Just when I think

Essie Sue's thought of it all, she dreams up another fund-raiser that will have us all running around like the Keystone Kops. She's determined to raise the funds for that totally superfluous Queen Esther statue in memory of her sister Marla. In marble, near the temple steps, yet. Better she should give the money to the food bank, but go tell her that. She says they're both good causes, and somebody else can be in charge of the other one.

Brace yourself for this. Under Essie Sue's prodding (make that electric prodding), the temple board voted fourteen to two to sell frozen six-packs of reduced-fat matzo balls throughout the community. You heard it here first. Buster Copeland and I were the only members to vote against the motion.

This was the annotated memo she mailed out before the vote—with Kevin's obvious help. I'd say it reflects a unique interpretation of Psalm 23.

## From Fund-Raising Chairperson Margolis to the Board

*Thou has anointed my head with oil, My cup runneth over.*

*As the Good Book clearly points out, ladies and gentlemen, oil is most blessedly used externally, not internally (see the Book of Psalms). Our bodies were not made to ingest huge quantities of fat (see the collected works of Jane E. Brody).*

*Therefore, as an example to the community, and in reflection of the principles of my health spa, the Center for Bodily Movement, I hereby endorse the concept of fat-free fund-raisers, or at the very least, reduced-fat. The First Annual Temple Matzo Ball Sale will feature the convenience of frozen, unsalted matzo balls made with vegetable oil instead of chicken schmaltz, sold in packs of six.*

Spirituality Unsaturated—*this is our motto and our mission.*

*Sincerely,*
*Essie Sue Margolis*

You remember Buster, don't you, Nan? His first comment at the board meeting was that without salt and fat, it *wasn't* a matzo ball. The sample Essie Sue brought in for taste-testing rated somewhere on a scale between *corrugated box* and *mattress innards*. Anyway, we lost the vote, the cooking began, and now there are six-packs of diet matzo balls stashed in freezers all over town, including The Hot Bagel and the spa kitchen.

The rabbi was rewarded for his help, though. She appointed him to represent the Temple on the interfaith baseball team I wrote you about. Something tells me this was not a kid who got picked first for the teams on the school playground, but he seems thrilled at this latest honor. Tomorrow night I'm meeting Kevin and Bogie—Essie Sue's trainer-turned-coach—at the spa to talk about team expenses. I'll keep you posted.

# 3

I dread these meetings with Kevin, even in the relatively public setting of the gym. He still thinks there's a chance I might add him to my spousal hit parade as Rabbi Number Two, in place of Rabbi Number One, deceased. I've tried to tell him it doesn't work that way. My husband, Stu, who was killed two and a half years ago, and whose murder was solved only last year with the help of his New York relatives and my e-mail pal, Nan, was Rabbi Kevin Kapstein's predecessor at the Temple. Two more opposite personalities could never be imagined. Stu was laid-back, and he related one to one, while Kevin is uptight, always on, and leans toward pleasing the crowd when he's not flattering his chief benefactor and matchmaker, Essie Sue. Needless to say, I'm not the least bit interested in replacing Kitselah, his former wife, who ran off with the proprietor of Manuel's Massage World before Kevin joined our congregation. I think she knew something.

Still, Kevin *is* the rabbi, I'm active around town and at the Temple, and I run into him a *lot*. Tonight is a good example. Milt Aboud, my partner at The Hot Bagel, is thrilled that I've brought in more business since he sold me a piece of the action, bagel-wise. He loves to think of me as the Outside partner—which is fine with me, since I don't keep baker's hours, and I'm glad I can help the business in other ways. When Essie Sue asked if our bagel bakery would sponsor the baseball team, my first thought was that I needed more contact with her like a hole in the head, but Milt decided the advertising would bring in customers, so here I am. Kevin wasn't on the team when I accepted, and I hadn't met Coach Bogie, either, believe me.

The gym closes at nine-thirty, and Kevin and I have arranged to meet just before closing time in the front lounge. That way, Bogie will be free to talk to us about the upcoming baseball season. I can't imagine he's busy being personal trainer to that many clients in a town this size, but who knows? Maybe Essie Sue has laid other duties on him besides the coaching. According to those who know him, the coaching's not a duty—the guy's a baseball nut, and fancies himself an overlooked Mark McGwire. He talks baseball endlessly, in readiness for the big moment, I guess.

I'm clutching my brown leather bomber jacket around

me as I hurry into the gym. The temperature plunged forty degrees today when a blue norther moved in unexpectedly. It was seventy-five degrees at noon—not unusual for March—and now it's in the mid-thirties. We're used to temperature extremes, but a mass of my yellow tulip bulbs just bloomed in the front yard, and I'm hoping they're hardy. At least it's not freezing.

I'm early for our meeting, and I look through the glass partitions into the exercise room. There's Kevin, in black shorts to his knees, black dress socks with white gym shoes, and a horizontally striped rugby shirt. One of the floor staff is helping him lift weights. I shudder to look. He's trying to push the bar over his head, but he's teetering, and the floor person is looking around wildly for assistance. One of the gym regulars rushes over to help steady him, and they're pointing at the clock. I think they're trying to tell him it's closing time.

Great—now I'm going to have to wait until he showers down. Just as I'm reaching for a fitness magazine, he appears—wearing the same getup, and heading toward me with his arms outstretched.

"Uh—Kevin," I say as I'm backing away, "don't you have to change clothes?"

"Rabbi Kapstein, Ruby. No, they told me the showers are closed for the night. I guess I'll just have to wait until I get home."

I ignore the Rabbi Kapstein remark as part of my ongoing campaign to bring him into the plane of ordinary mortals. I don't think a first-name basis with the widow of a colleague is what one could call getting too familiar. It's ludicrous, considering that I'm standing here a mere foot away from a rank body covered in sweat.

"You know, Kevin, it's possible that Bogie could think this is unhealthy behavior for a team member."

"You think so?" Kevin is in awe of Bogie. I understand they've even gone camping together. Kevin doesn't know from camping, but he's learning, and under Bogie's tutelage, I don't envy him.

"Let me do most of the talking tonight, Ruby. You know Bogie's a man's man." Oh, yeah, like I really want to be a part of whatever scintillating guy talk goes on between those two.

"Kevin, we're here to discuss whether or not you got overcharged for baseball uniforms. I don't think this has worldwide implications."

"I'm trained in public speaking. I know how to put things. You can learn from me, too, Ruby—you know I've offered to spend more time with you."

The hairs on the back of my neck are tingling, but fortunately, he's headed in another direction right now.

"I don't want Bogie thinking we're cheap. I represent the Margolis family interests here, too."

"Well, I represent The Hot Bagel interest, which comes to more than Milt and I had in mind for our share. Why *are* you representing Essie Sue, now that I think of it?"

"As the temple representative. I told her I'd take care of it, since Bogie listens to me."

I'll bet he does.

"Where is Bogie, by the way? I thought we set up this late meeting because he was working."

"One of his clients canceled. He's at batting practice in back."

"Batting practice? How come you're not there with the rest of them?"

He gives me the familiar condescending smile.

"I told you this is not something you'd understand, Ruby. Essie Sue has bought an automated machine for our batting practice. Bogie practices regularly. You didn't know the semi-pros were interested in him, I'll bet."

"She'd better not charge us for half of it." Bogie must be smarter than I thought if he's talked her into this.

"She's charging this up to gym equipment, and we're getting the benefit. Bogie's told her she can expand into a training facility with all his contacts in the baseball world."

I don't want to go there. What's more, I don't want to be here. It's late and I just want to get home. Soon.

"How do you get to the back of this place?" I'm thinking Kevin's going to freeze out there in his wet condition, but I can't worry about it. I throw on my jacket and head in the direction he's pointing. I hope they have lights.

I shouldn't have worried. As we go through the kitchen that Essie Sue renovated, and step out the back door, we're bathed in light. Ebbets Field in its heyday was never this bright. The gym's backyard is huge, and enclosed on all four sides with a high wooden fence—for privacy, Bogie says. I've never been out here before, but it looks freshly graded, with new turf put down. If the space were a bit larger, the team could use it as a stadium. She's obviously bought the whole package. I guess it's not that much of a leap from Queen Esther statues to this.

We go through a gate to the backyard, which has been fitted out in professional style—if you happen to be a baseball pro. It's true that my eyes are seeing only dollar signs, but even an objective viewer would gasp at this setup. Dominating the field is a huge black steel contraption mounted on a tripod. Large concave drive wheels are attached to electronic equipment that seems to be controlled by assorted dials, knobs, and switches.

"That pitching machine costs over seventeen hundred dollars," Kevin announces, "and it's used by all the major league baseball teams. Isn't it great? It's electronically spin balanced, and it can pitch fastballs, curves, and sliders at up to ninety-five miles per hour."

"You need this for practice? From what I saw, your baseball team is strictly sandlot status."

"You don't get it."

Apparently, I don't. Even Ted Turner would think twice about buying this contraption. It must weigh over a hundred pounds.

"You've got to be with it today, Ruby. Bogie says this is for our future growth, and electronics is the way to go. This has an automatic feeder that can load four hundred balls."

"Uh-huh. I can see this for Yankee Stadium, Kevin, but what can you possibly do with four hundred balls?" An awful thought hits me. "Don't tell me you actually bought four hundred balls?"

"You wouldn't understand. I don't know why Milt put you on this committee. He should have had a man."

He should have had a millionaire. The big machine has

spawned offspring—I see several smaller setups to the left and right.

"Those are soft-toss stations, where we learn coordination by hitting into nets around the field. And these are the batting tees, where the beginners hit. Bogie says we have to work our way up to the big one."

"How many people have worked their way up to the seventeen-hundred-dollar deal?"

"Only Bogie, so far."

Okay, I now have a pretty good picture of what's going on here. Essie Sue deserves this, but it's way too rich for The Hot Bagel's blood. I'm glad I saw this before we sprang for overpriced uniforms. They're probably expensive knockoffs of NASA space suits, at two thou a throw.

"So where's the big man?" I'm not looking forward to this.

"Maybe he's looking for balls. He hits lots of home runs over the fence into the woods."

"With four hundred balls on hand, why would he need to look for them?" I'm imagining the waste, and already picturing some big substitute egg hunt where Essie Sue has half the town combing the woods for lost baseballs.

"I'm only waiting a few more minutes, Kevin. The wind's up, if you hadn't noticed, and I'm ready to turn in."

"But all the lights are still on out here. I know he's around. I'd call him, but it's so windy out here, he'd never hear me."

We're headed back the other way, toward the gate, when Kevin's face brightens.

"There he is—he's taking time-out. I was expecting to see him standing up and swinging."

"I don't know from taking time-out. What are you talking about?"

"You probably got to the gym late and he got tired of waiting."

"You were the one we were waiting for, if you remember."

"What do you mean, me? I didn't even take time to shower."

"Stow it, Kevin. Just tell me where he's gone for the time-out—whatever the hell that is."

"Don't let Bogie hear you cursing, Ruby. He's right over there. He's resting from his practice—next to the batting station."

"Resting? It's freezing out here, and there's not a bench in sight."

"No bench. He's on the ground. On his back. He's napping.

"Bogie? Bogie?" Kevin's voice is tenuous. He's fidgeting beside me, apparently waiting for me to do something. It figures.

I finally shift my eyes downward to a man on the grass, partially hidden from my view by two catch nets tied together to make a backstop for balls. I run over and drop on my knees to the ground.

Bogie, stretched out on his back with the pole of a batting tee lying near his face, is definitely not napping.

This is the first time I've *ever* seen Essie Sue rumpled. She's thrown on a pair of blue jeans (who knew she even had jeans?) with a slightly less than pressed silk blouse under a black wool dress coat, and she's standing shivering in the midnight wind with the rest of us.

"I already put my winter clothes in the cedar closet—who knew, so close to Passover?" She's glaring at me as if it's my fault she had to be dragged from her bed to a backyard that's fast taking on a circus atmosphere. Lieutenant Paul Lundy's here with his entire crew—he's the great guy who helped me live through our bagel bakery murder with my sanity intact. The Center for Bodily Movement is now a crime scene in addition to its other functions, and Essie Sue is not amused.

"Don't look at me," I warn her, "the rabbi saw the body first." I'm hoping Kevin's title will deflect attention from me.

Poor Kevin is sitting cross-legged on the grass, in his black gym shorts, yet. I don't think he even feels the cold—the shock of Bogie's death is just hitting him. These two were such an odd couple, mismatched in every way, but my instinct tells me there's a simple answer for the connection. Bogie was probably the first jock ever to show an interest in Kevin.

"I told the police I have no idea why or how Bogie died, Ruby." Kevin's practically wailing now. "I still can't believe he's not going to wake up."

"Do you know who any of his friends were?"

"You're not going to interrogate me, too, are you?"

Now I'm feeling guilty. Seeing Bogie like that was a shock for me. Even though I didn't really know him like Kevin did, I never thought I'd be seeing him dead. It brings back a lot of pain for me from my own experiences with Stu's death, and when I'm trying to deny that, I get a little hyperactive.

"Well, no, not now, Kevin, but I'm just curious. You hung out with him a little bit, didn't you? Maybe you can tell me later."

"Quit picking on the rabbi, Ruby." Essie Sue's his mouthpiece all of a sudden.

I hate being ganged up on. "Look, you two, I've been interrogated, too, remember? And I *really* didn't know

Bogie. But Kevin did. He can probably be a big help to the police."

"I've arranged for him to see the police tomorrow, when he's feeling better." Essie Sue is trying to help Kevin up off the ground and order me around at the same time. "You can fill them in for now."

"Thanks a bunch." I'm exhausted, but to be honest, I don't want to leave just yet. I want to see what Paul Lundy thinks happened. And I'm always better off when Essie Sue and Kevin are out of my hair.

It's rubber-glove city out here. I try to snag Paul, who's kneeling by the body, surrounded by people filling up various plastic bags.

"Paul, that plastic yellow batting tee looks awfully lightweight to be a weapon."

He looks up and gives me a grin. Maybe it's a smirk—I'm not sure.

"A couple of murders under your belt and you're a pro, huh, Ruby?"

Now I'm insulted. I guess it was a smirk. He points to the practice tee, a waist-high tube, scooped out on top so that a ball can rest in the hollow, ready to bat. It lies near the baseball bat Bogie was using.

"Actually, these are made of a pretty strong polyurethane," he says. "But you didn't look at the base—it's made of steel as a counterweight, and one side of the base is pointed. It could do a nasty job."

I have very thick skin when I'm trying to be a pro, so I ignore his brush-off and forge ahead.

"But that's my point—it's not that nasty."

Paul gets up and walks me away from the body.

"We don't know how it happened yet, so take it easy. You'd be surprised what surfaces in lab work. He could have ingested something toxic and fallen on some equipment, or he could have died from natural causes and done the same. It looks as though he suffered a blow to the head of some type."

"Something toxic? Maybe he ate one of Essie Sue's diet matzo balls and dropped dead. She's been making the staff taste samples on breaks."

"Spare me. Don't forget she knows all of us from the investigation into her sister's killing. She's already made a pilgrimage to the station and extracted pledges from all of us to buy matzo balls—even the rookies are down for a carton."

"She's relentless—they should be warned to stay away from her. You look tired, Paul. Do you have to be here all night?"

"An hour more should do it—then I get to go home, too."

"Have you ruled out the batting tee as a weapon?"

"I told you it's too early to tell. Someone could have come out here and hit him with the batting tee. Or with another bat they ran off with. That's why you and the rabbi are important, and so are the few people in the gym who were here late. We have to find out who saw him alive last."

"Do you want me to stick around?"

"I want you not to stick around. You've answered a lot of questions already, and frankly, you're looking pale. Go home and go to bed."

"You don't think I can sleep now?"

"Maybe not, but you can lie down and get warm. Do you want me to have someone drive you home?"

"I'm fine."

Fine, I'm not, but I manage to keep my shaky hands on the wheel all the way home. I think the norther's passed through—the weather seems warmer even though it's almost two in the morning. The roses in my front yard are about to bloom, and the tulips are holding their own. Reminders that some things are still very much alive.

Oy Vay's waiting for me in the backyard, and am I glad to wrap my arms around her when we get inside. Oy Vay's my three-legged golden retriever and sole housemate now that Stu's gone and our son Joshie's all grown up.

Regardless of recent experience, I don't see dead men every day, and I can't sleep, even with the help of some cognac I've had in the house for a couple of years now and decided to break out tonight.

I'm nice and warm, as I lie here on my back and stare at the ceiling. I can visualize the whole scene Kevin and I saw in the backyard of the gym, when we first walked outside, centuries ago at nine-thirty.

There's only one problem with my idyllic vision of a man's batting practice, before the dead body, before the swarms of forensics. It was green and it was quiet, except for the wind. But there were no balls on the ground. Not one. Not anywhere.

# 5

"People, we need a concept for the matzo ball sales."

"I take it you have one," I say in my capacity as one of the two people Essie Sue is addressing.

The lunch rush is over at The Hot Bagel, but we're crowded around a tiny circular table by the window. It's too small, but Essie Sue thinks round tables have a more "familial" feeling. Family, we'll never be. My partner, Milt, is sitting here glaring, having originally refused to come over and pour refills—probably a wise move, since he's not to be trusted with a pot of scalding coffee anywhere near our mutual nemesis. I persuaded him to join us when

Essie Sue hinted she had news of Bogie's death—he's as curious as I am.

She's dropped in after lunch because she knows this is my time at the bakery and I'll be a captive audience. I do my work here in the afternoon—which means Milt's old bakery workers have plenty of time to test my limits. Bradley Axelrod and Carol Sealy, baker and cashier, have yet to get used to the change in management.

I'm now discovering that Essie Sue got us to the table under false pretenses—she knows nothing about the police investigation. Her "news" turned out to be an advance article from our local weekly, *The Eternal Ear* (motto: nose to the grindstone; ear to the ground), reporting offhandedly that a man had been found dead in the backyard of the former Sam's Gym. The Center for Bodily Movement, the *Ear*'s biggest advertiser, was not mentioned. Chalk one up to Essie Sue—she's obviously intimidated the editor.

She is, in fact, distancing herself remarkably from the death of someone she used to rave about. Now Bogie is only an unfortunate employee who happened to expire on the premises, and she's hoping everyone will forget the whole thing. Not me—I keep remembering last night's scene, and all my buttons are pushed. We gave interviews at the station house this morning, but I know there's also been a lot of police activity at the gym, and I've been hounding Essie Sue for some real information. She only wants to talk *concepts*.

"People, you know how the frequent flier programs

have travel partners? For this project, we're looking for Diet Partners. My Center is the fitness capital of the area. It only takes a small leap to umbrella in all the reducing outfits in Austin. They can work with us to help sales and promote themselves."

"Umbrella in? What in the hell are you talking about? And is this gonna cost me any money?" Milt's zero tolerance for Essie Sue doesn't leave much maneuvering room.

"I guess she's talking about networking," I say, realizing with horror that, compared to "networking," I actually *prefer* "umbrella in."

Milt snorts, heading for the kitchen, and I'm left carrying on the conversation.

"We'll all learn more about this later," she says cryptically. I don't think I want to know what she means.

"Ruby, the bakery looks much better," she says.

Uh-oh. She must want something big if she's resorting to flattery. She's got an eye for fashion, but my plans for The Hot Bagel were hardly what I'd call chic. I'd persuaded Milt to put some bookshelves on the bare walls, and had no trouble whatsoever filling them up. My attic was overflowing with Stu's fiction and my travel books, for starters, along with volumes I'd been saying since childhood I ought to give away. They stuck to my hands whenever I even thought of getting rid of them—obviously, some curse I was born with.

Customers in the bakery love the books, even though most of them just get glanced at. We put a few secondhand easy chairs in strategic places alongside end tables so people could balance their coffee cups, and that did it.

For practically no money whatsoever, The Hot Bagel was transformed.

"You've given the place some warmth, Ruby. It looked like a bathroom before." True to form, Essie Sue's never produced a compliment without its accompanying *utz:* the verbal jab that goes with it. At least Milt's not close enough to catch that one.

"Gee, thanks. I thought you didn't approve of a former rabbi's wife selling bagels."

"That's another issue, dear. I'm strictly talking decorating. Besides, I never see you selling bagels. What do you do here?"

"The books, the buying, the upkeep, and the marketing. Milt handles the help and the day-to-day operations." Why am I telling her *any* of this—it's none of her business. She has a way of getting things out of me before I can remember I'm a grown-up. And she always manages to use it against me.

"I'm having an expanded committee meeting this week at Temple, and I'm counting on you to come, Ruby. As a business consultant."

Yep, it's happening already.

"What committee?"

"The Marble Arts Section of the Temple Beautification Committee." *Her* marbles aren't any too secure when it comes to her dead sister Marla's statue, but the project is nevertheless proceeding at an alarming pace.

"You mean you want my professional services? Are you planning to computerize the operation?" That'll be the day.

"You'd take money for temple work?" She looks horrified.

I know when I'm licked, but I'm not going quietly.

"Why do you want me there? You know I have the influence of a gnat at these meetings."

"I need every head I can get. It's hard to attract people to meetings in the spring. They go outside."

"Oh."

I don't know what else to say to this, and I notice my silence is making her uncomfortable. She's probably wondering if she's got me nailed down yet.

She taps the hammer one more time for good measure.

"Well, it's not just that you're filling a chair. It's prestigious."

"Huh?"

"It's good for the committee to have the rabbi's wife there."

I have to hand it to her. This is BS at its finest. From floor space to prestige in one breath.

"Even if you're only a dead rabbi's wife—not a real one."

Hah! I knew she couldn't sustain it. Time for my final terms.

"I'll be at the committee meeting, but only if you do something for me."

"Yeah, what?" She gives me the look. The veneer's off, but at least we're both more comfortable.

"The police are swarming all over the gym. Find out what's really going on, Essie Sue. I can't just hang out at the police station—even if I was one of the people who discovered the body."

"I'll keep you posted as things come up."

"Not good enough. Your committee meets next week, right?"

"Okay," she says. "I'll start asking questions now. Discreetly."

E-mail from: Ruby
To: Nan
Subject: *Pushed the Right Buttons*

I got some information—Essie Sue went for my tit-for-tat deal, and came through with some gossip—so now she's interested in her own right—ha. There's no way I could have pestered Lieutenant Paul Lundy for this—he's tight as a drum when he wants to be.

The back of the gym has been cordoned off and no one can get through, but Essie Sue says investigators are still in and out of the area. They hang out in the Center kitchen for coffee, and she hears things—just rumors at this point. They're doing some tests on the batting machine, which certainly makes sense, since a baseball could have accidentally hit him between the eyes. I told you that's where the wound is, didn't I? She doesn't think the autopsy showed anything internal, like stroke or poison, which might have caused him to fall on something sharp, although some of those tests take a while to come back. No undigested matzo balls killed him, either! Not that Essie Sue would let evidence of *that* kind cross her lips. She's about to rain matzo balls all over Eternal, and she's not brooking interference from a mere death in her own backyard.

I'm most interested in the accident theory, although when I work it out in my mind, none of the scenarios hold up. If someone were pitching for him, then I can see the wild-ball possibility, but not with an expensive machine like that. And as I said before, where are the balls? I didn't see a one near the body, though of course it was dark. Still, floodlights were all over the place.

The All Faiths Baseball Team has been put on indefinite hold, by the way. I don't think Kevin cares—he's too upset over Bogie's death.

Take good notes on criminal law. In case this was a murder, I want to have my own expert on hand.

E-mail from: Nan
To: Ruby
Subject: *Sniff Around*

Don't depend on my expertise for *anything*—I feel that I'm barely keeping afloat. Working for a lawyer definitely didn't help me on law school exams—they're a different breed altogether. My accounting courses in college were easier for me than this stuff—they were at least straightforward. And I minored in English Lit., where you could throw a lot of bull if you were good at it. Here, though, they want the buckshot approach. You're supposed to think of all the different issues you could possibly bring up to attack the opponent's theory, and you can leave the well-crafted prose for appellate court briefs.

Why aren't you questioning the rabbi about this guy? Never mind—I know the answer to that. But I think you ought to overcome your resistance, and get him talking about Bogie.

The Temple Beautification Committee, Marble Arts Section, is meeting in the temple boardroom—not the Blumberg Social Hall or the Levy Patio, but the boardroom. In the realm of Eternal Jewish geopolitics, this means big time.

Essie Sue has done her homework, and twenty leading lights are more or less voluntarily assembled.

"Ladies and gentlemen, we need to get down to business. The whole town is awaiting the outcome of our deliberations."

"Save it for the press release, Essie Sue. I see this is gonna be a long night."

Brother Copeland, turned out identically to his brother

Buster in boots, button-down, and chinos, is waving the committee agenda in one hand and a stopwatch in the other. "I'm timing everybody, and the hook's aimed for you first."

"You may monitor each speaker, but the chair is excepted." Ignoring the "Like hell" emanating from Brother's side of the conference table, Essie Sue points to me.

"Ruby Rothman, along with my husband Hal and myself, will judge your nominations for our fund-raising Diet Partners. We need these partners to help spread our spiritual and nutritional message."

"You mean you need them to help sell the matzo balls," Brother says.

"Well, that, too." Essie Sue's not budging. "I want each of you, in your own words, to tell us why you think your particular food control organization will meet our needs."

"What exactly *are* our needs?" That's Buster, egged on by Brother to his left.

"*Utzes* are not welcome." Essie Sue gives him a look. "Our requirements are to choose the perfect vehicles to endorse our diet matzo balls and pass the word along. I already have a couple of Diet Partners in the works, but we need more—that's where the committee members can be helpful. Merlina Margolis will lead off."

Merlina is Hal's niece. *Oy*. Assembling this motley crew must have been like pulling teeth if Essie Sue's had to reach this far into the barrel. Merlina's on the dramatic side—she opens with a tear in her voice.

"Like before I discovered Diet Warehouse, I thought all TV dinners were, you know, like disgusting frozen fried chicken skin. But no. Diet Warehouse TV dinners are like your whole new life in a box, people." Uh-oh—I know who rehearsed *her*.

"Canned juices, salad dressing packets, diet desserts—they're all in your weekly allotment. And the people there will help you carry three or four heavy bags out to your car every week. It's all the groceries you need for a healthy life, except of course the fresh lettuce and veggies and fruit and stuff you need to buy at your regular grocery. Plus you get to report to your counselor for a fee. And for that same fee you get to buy all this stuff, people. And they'll *let* you lose pounds for dollars."

Wow. In biblical times, you could get married for twenty shekels and a cow. Now we're paying strangers for the privilege of losing part of our own bodies. What a deal.

"Point of order!" It's Dollie Leventhal. "This is highway robbery—at Snackers with No Names we get to lose weight for free. And it's totally secret. Why, I can look around me at this very table and point out people who've lost over and over again."

"Thank you, Dollie, but let's hold your point for later. Our niece hasn't finished."

"She's history!" Brother's waving his stopwatch.

"Hold it, Brother." Buster's on his feet. "I lost seven pounds at Scale Gazers, and I didn't have to lose my dignity to do it."

"You might be my flesh and blood, Buster," Brother says, "but you been going for a hellava long time for just seven pounds."

"But they clapped for every one of those damned

pounds, and I'm proud of it. We clap for each other after we stand in line to get weighed down and hear the lecture of the week. Then we look at the new products. And maybe qualify to buy a string of advance admission coupons to save money. I'm not sure how much we save because we have to pay even if we don't go. The weeks we don't go, we might be cheating—you know—eating. So we have to pay for that. Makes sense to me."

Let's see now. Would I rather pay my own dollars for my own pounds at the first place, or pay money for not coming at this place? Dollars for not coming, hands down. Makes sense to me.

Sally Handover rises unbidden, but Essie Sue lets her speak. "My practitioner, Teddy, uses a much kinder, gentler approach. He lets you fill up your kitchen with everything you've ever wanted—hot fudge sauce, fresh pecans, triple-rich Häagen-Dazs, rib roast, sour cream, hot biscuits and butter—"

At this point, the whole room is leaning forward with more interest than I've seen all night. Sally's taking control now.

"Teddy says you have to get being deprived out of your system first. If you have everything you want in the same room with you, you'll relax and not feel you have to eat it all before it disappears. You'll pick and choose."

"So did you?" That's Mr. Chernoff's voice from the end of the table.

"Did I what—pick and choose? Yes, every session, I make a list for Teddy of all the wonderful things I relax with."

"So did you?" Mr. Chernoff asks again.

"I told you—"

"Did you lose weight?"

"It's a process, Mr. Chernoff." Sally's rolling her eyes heavenward—apparently at his lack of sophistication. "I'm in the relaxing half now."

"So relax. But did you lose?"

"I gained. But that's to be expected for now."

You can say that again. With triple-rich Häagen-Dazs, I'd definitely expect it.

Another voice heard from—Steve Coperman. "My shrink says it's all in your mind. The fat isn't real in the psychic sense—it's like a visible coagulation of your wants, needs, and desires all rolled into one."

Well, he got the coagulation right. And, boy, do I wish it weren't real. While we're digesting that one, the door to the boardroom flies open. Myrna Hurst and her sister Henrietta burst in, carrying picket signs—WE LOVE GIRTH and ZEALOUS FOR ZAFTIGS. Essie Sue is not amused.

"Out!" she yells. "This is by invitation only."

"We think you should have sunrise-sunset laws—or whatever," the sisters pipe up.

Looks like they're on to something.

"Let 'em stay, Essie Sue," Buster says. "Aren't we an open-meeting kind of place?"

She nods okay to Buster, then glares at me. "Where's the parliamentarian?"

Buster points to one of the chairs. The parliamentarian looks a little peaked.

"She's fasting," Brother says. "That's her weight-loss

method. She was supposed to report on the experience later."

I think we'd better let the Yom Kippur diet pass—I don't think this woman's going to make it.

It's time to proceed, so I take advantage of the parliamentarian's disability. "I move to adjourn and take the other nominations in writing. All in favor?"

Essie Sue's having none of it. "Hey, you're not in control here—I am."

I've got the jump on her, though, because all hands fly up.

"We can't adjourn yet—we haven't heard from the fat-burns-fat people, the think-thin people, or the handwriting experts."

Handwriting experts? I rescind my motion. We hear the fat-fats, the think-thins, and Dorothy Doney, the handwriting expert.

"You write four hundred 'd's' in rows of twenty, four times a day. I swear it trains your brain not to want food. You can look this up."

I see Essie Sue jotting down her first notes of the evening—I don't think she's ever heard of the handwriting deal. Although Essie Sue is a woman no fat cell would dare approach, believe me, she's not taking any chances.

# 7

I fool around in the rest room until Essie Sue and her committee are safely out of the Temple. Although nothing would please me more than to spend the rest of the evening reading in bed after that exhausting tour of Fat City, I find myself heading down the corridor to Kevin's study. I'm dying to find out if he knows anything about Bogie's past. Essie Sue excused him from the meeting since he was teaching his weekly Conversion to Judaism class tonight. From what I've heard of that conversion class, I just hope there's more traffic in than out of it—he's not exactly known for his pulpit-side manner. Kevin scared Sarah Glassberg's fiancé off the first night by telling him he had to read Genesis, Exodus, and half of Leviticus before the next meeting, to catch up with the rest of the class.

A young couple is leaving as I reach the door of the study. Kevin's giving some parting advice.

"Don't forget, Bob—just tell your mother the rabbi said it wasn't a good idea for you to help her plan the nieces' Easter egg hunt this year. Blame it on me—she'll respect an authority figure."

*Oy*. I can see Judeo-Christian relations going down the tubes as I stand here. Bob doesn't look any too happy—not to mention the probable fiancée. At any rate, she's bawling him out.

"It's your own fault for telling him about the weekend," she says. "Why couldn't you keep your mouth shut?"

"But he's a rabbi. It's like a priest, right? They know everything."

"Not about the glazed ham, he doesn't."

I smile politely and let them pass, trying not to think about Bob's family members flattened like bowling pins from the force of Kevin's directives.

"Hi—do you have a minute?"

"Ruby—for you, I'll even overlook your not having an appointment."

Gee, that's a break. Do I thank him?

For a while, I couldn't go into the large temple study—it reminded me too much of Stu. But Kevin, with the help of the decorating committee, chaired by we-know-who, has transformed the place, and now I don't even associate it with my husband. Not that he'd be caught dead in it, you should excuse the expression.

The old study had a workspace in the corner, with an ancient roll-top Stu had inherited from his father, and a long table coming out from the desk in an L-shape. He wasn't the neatest guy—that table held papers that hadn't seen the light of day in five years, and the whole unruly space was stuck over in the part of the room where Stu worked when he was alone. The rest of his office looked like a living room—two sofas and three or four comfortable chairs circling a big oak coffee table, and that was where he lived and read and rested and had his friends drop by.

A lot of friends stopped in to schmooze from time to time—kids, adults—most of them congregants, and the rest from all over the place—Eternal, Austin, the university, the park. Some didn't smell too good, but all were welcome. Except when people had private matters to discuss or groups were meeting, the rule was pretty much open house. Chaotic, but effective, and an awful lot got done that couldn't be cataloged.

The first thing Essie Sue did when Kevin was selected was to give everything to the thrift shop. Except for the desk, which I brought home, all the furniture belonged to the Temple. She hated it—each and every piece—and she'd been trying to get her hands on the stuff for years with no luck.

"It's not dignified." That refrain was the overwhelming favorite, but there were worse. "It's so schleppy for a representative of the Jewish people" was another. Stu hadn't argued with her—he'd just said hands off.

"Everything else in the building is subject to democratic

vote," he would tell her, "but just think of my space as a little autocracy." She couldn't budge him, even when she carefully brushed off the furniture before she sat down.

But that was then, and this is unmistakably now. Although appointmentless, I'm welcomed to Kevin's world. He's sitting behind what I can only describe as the ship of state—a massive mahogany desk with gilded rosettes, anchored to the center of the room. Napoleon would feel right at home here. Kevin occupies a huge brown leather throne, and directs me to one of the circle of tiny chairs radiating from the desk front. No wonder Bob felt compelled to spill his guts—that glazed ham is history.

"I don't believe you've seen my new glass and stainless steel credenza." He points toward a crystalline structure rising from the former coffee table area like a winged phoenix.

"What's it for?" I'm transfixed.

"It's decorative. Doesn't it look like something right out of *Architectural Digest*?"

All is revealed. I don't even have to ask who ordered *this*.

"I wanted the room to make a statement."

It makes a statement all right. *Ongepotchket*. That's Yiddish for what happens when you mix rococo with the Bauhaus.

"I don't see any books or journals here. Aren't we supposed to be the People of the Book?"

"The books are behind these panels—clever, yes? Essie Sue wanted them to be neat and organized, not like . . ."

"Not like the former occupant of the room?"

"Look, Ruby, it's well known we had different styles. From what I've heard of your husband's library, it was, to put it bluntly, a dust-catcher—books overflowing all over the place."

"Yeah, a real shame." I look up at him from my lowly perch beneath the desk from on high, and I wonder how Stu would react to the invisible bookshelves. Snort, probably.

"Wanna see my computer? I'm a power user. It's in back of this panel."

"It's been great, but I really stopped by to ask if you could tell me anything more about Bogie."

I see his jaw slacken a bit before he hides behind his own invisible panels. I'm heartened—at least there's something still in there.

"I don't mean to stir up old feelings, Kevin. I just thought we could talk about who Bogie was—you knew him better than any of us did."

"He was a great guy, Ruby. People thought he was tough, but he was very nice when you knew him."

"Was he happy here in Eternal?"

"He said he had trouble meeting girls here—he thought they were snobs. He wasn't all that thrilled with his job, either, but don't tell Essie Sue."

I'm thinking she won't be able to do anything to him now, but I keep going. "You mean after all that fabulous sports equipment, he wasn't satisfied here?"

"They had some run-ins. She thought the sports equipment would bring a lot of professionals to the gym. I guess that was partly Bogie's fault—he wanted the stuff so badly that he might have oversold the idea. People didn't exactly flock there to practice, and Essie Sue blamed him for sticking her with the bills. His salary wasn't great, either."

I'll bet. Of course, to the rest of us, Essie Sue made Bogie sound like a prize. I guess she still had hopes he'd bring in some business. Kevin seems genuinely affected, and I can't help thinking he knows something that can help the investigation.

"So was he looking around?"

"Looking around where?"

"For a job."

Kevin's fidgeting with the pens on his desk. I'm on to something.

"It could be important, Kevin. If he was a friend of yours, you owe it to him."

"He made me promise, Ruby. I can't tell what his plans were. He'd have died if he'd thought Essie Sue would find out."

"He did die, Kevin. And there's no reason Essie Sue has to know you told me about any of this. The police investigate leads all over the community. If someone offered him a position, they'll discover it eventually. We're just making their job easier. Besides, don't think they won't question you again just because they asked for some preliminary facts. This way, they'll already have this information."

"Okay." He stands up.

"Kevin, either sit back in your chair or come down here with the peasants. When you stand up at your desk like that, I feel as though you're in the pulpit giving me a sermon."

I'm hoping he'll come down, but he slumps back in his seat, and I'm left looking up at him again. No wonder I hear congregants aren't dropping in as much—you could get a pain in the neck from these visits.

"You know that guest ranch twenty miles from Eternal that those movie people built?"

"You mean Fit and Rural? Central Texas's newest claim to fame for the healthy wealthy? I even applied to submit a bid for customizing their software. In fact, I think Essie Sue nominated them for a matzo ball partner."

"Diet Partner—that's what she calls it, Ruby. Bogie was against it—he said they're too big-time for something like that. And of course he didn't want her anywhere near the place while he was angling for a real job—they'd only given him a part-time one."

"Of course, we don't know they're so big-time, do we? And no one's really said which movie stars bought it. What did they want Bogie for?"

"Maybe athletic director. It would have been *huge,* he said. Although it made me nervous knowing about it—I want to keep on the good side of her."

A side she keeps fairly well hidden most of the time—but let Kevin keep his illusions.

"Did Bogie know the managers?"

"Yes, the Poundburns. Hetty and Harmon. You must know them, too, if you applied to do their software."

"The Poundburns? Gimme a break. Nobody would make up that name."

"He said it was their real name. Like Poundstone—that's not made up."

"But that's different . . ." I realize whom I'm talking to, and keep on course. "In answer to your question, Kevin—

no, I never met the managers. They never asked me out there to talk about a bid, either. I answered an ad in the paper a month or so ago."

I make a mental note to talk to Paul Lundy about the Poundburns, if I can keep a straight face. Or maybe I can call about the application.

"Too bad you didn't know Bogie then. Maybe he could have gotten you the job."

"Yeah, too bad. Did he ever talk about his life before he moved here?"

"Well, you know all about his Mr. Muscle title—he got lots of publicity on that. Essie Sue was really impressed. Maybe she still has some of his clippings."

Hey, a real live tip. "Not bad, Kevin—I'll ask her. All she showed me was the employment application she gave the police. Can you call me with anything else that comes to mind?"

"Sure. I've been wanting to call you."

He descends from on high before I can jump up, and leans over my chair.

"Will you go out with me on another date?"

"Another date?"

"Well, we had the date for the temple fund-raising dance."

How quickly we repress. I'm know I'm in denial about the dance from hell, but the one thing I do remember was that it was *not* a date. Still, he's given me a tip about Bogie, so I let it go at that and jump up from my chair, bumping both our noses in the process.

What I'll do for clues.

# 8

When I'm up early on Sunday mornings, I like to take Oy Vay to the park. Traffic is nonexistent—the parishioners are home having pancakes before dressing up for the stately ride downtown. Eternal's most established churches are still near the old town square, where they flourish among gardens as well tended as their owners. East of town, where I live on Watermelon Lane, all the nonpraying gardeners skipping church are on their knees solely to dig. We're diggin' fools on Watermelon Lane, especially since the sun's out today. Oy Vay, of course, wants to help, which is why we're involved in such a tug-of-war on our way home from the sandpiles and other burrowing opportunities.

I'm pulling on the leash to keep Oy Vay from helping my next-door neighbor, Mrs. Chen, dig up old roots from last year, when I see a car parked in my driveway. Two cars, actually. One is Essie Sue's silver Lincoln Continental, and dwarfing even that is Kevin's enormous midnight blue minivan. I'm flabbergasted. When I tell you it's early, I'm talking in the eight o'clock range.

They're so wrapped up in their own conversation, they don't even see us cutting across the lawn from the other side of the house, which is fine with me. I head toward the back door with Oy Vay loping beside me, having finally given up her root quest. She's barked at every bird in sight on the way home, so she doesn't seem interested in greeting our visitors in the driveway. Maybe they'll leave and I can go back to sleep, which I had fully intended to do after our long romp in the park.

No such luck.

"Ruby!"

She's sent Kevin running around back, in a coat and tie, yet.

"Let us in. Didn't you see us?"

"Why should I expect cars in my driveway at this hour?" I realize that if anyone else had parked there except these two, I'd be worried somebody had died.

"Essie Sue's waiting at the front door to be let in."

"So I hear." The doorbell's ringing nonstop. I decide I don't want to hear the purpose of this visit twice, so I don't ask Kevin. I'm banging the coffeepot around, determined to grind my beans so I can at least keep awake with Sumatra if it's impossible to sleep.

Kevin's still standing at the back door. "Aren't you going to answer the bell?"

"No."

He runs through the kitchen to the front door, giving Oy Vay a wide berth. He needn't worry. She used to greet these two with her usual joyful exuberance, but now she doesn't like them anymore. This is no dumb animal.

"Ruby, this is outrageous."

"You can say that again."

"It's an emergency, Ruby." Essie Sue's face is actually perspiring under the blush.

"I imagine you didn't bother to call first, either."

"We didn't need to call. Where on earth would you be at eight o'clock on Sunday morning? Who knew you'd be out already?"

I give the Sumatra an extra grind for good measure.

"Let's all sit down around the table and wait for the coffee," Kevin says. "I'm sure Ruby has some good bagels from the bakery, too."

"You're out of luck. It's coffee or nothing."

Essie Sue looks scandalized. "I've always told you a rabbi's wife should keep drop-in food around, just in case."

"Former rabbi's wife. I have anchovies."

"Kevin, I hate for you to have to hear this." Essie Sue leans over and puts her hands over his ears. I chuckle before I realize she's serious. "I'm sure Ruby's hostessing skills could be brought up to speed in no time with the right motivation."

"Enough catastrophizing, Essie Sue. What's the emergency?"

"The Eternal Ministerial Council has just put the Jews in charge of the annual spring Interfaith Event. It was the Unitarians' turn this year, but they backed out—I don't have to remind you that chaos is their middle name. I've tried to tell them for years that a few Fig Newtons and some Kool-Aid do *not* an elegant reception make, but it's fallen on dead ears."

"Deaf ears," Kevin corrects. Big mistake.

"When I say dead, I mean dead. Wait'll *you* have to deal with people, some of them former temple members, I might add, who don't know a sermon from a lecture."

"Or maybe they do," I say.

"Rabbi, don't listen to Ruby. She has a soft spot for the Unitarians."

This is my cue. "So why *are* we listening to Ruby in Ruby's kitchen at eight o'clock on a Sunday morning?"

"Because of my great idea." Uh-oh. If Kevin's this excited, I need to worry. Oy Vay warns me with a look before wandering out of the kitchen.

"I was trying to figure out how we could host the interfaith gathering at about the same time we're putting on the temple Passover Seder. Then it came to me. We can have an Ecumenical Seder this year. I called Essie Sue and she not only loved my idea, she expanded on it."

A lethal combo if I've ever heard one. At least the coffee's ready—maybe the caffeine kick will diffuse the sense of dread I'm experiencing.

Essie Sue's beaming. "This rabbi thinks on a big scale," she tells me. "This is leadership with a capital *L*." Another dig at Stu—who was long on substance, short on style.

"So is this good or bad for the Jews—or more specifically, is it gonna be good or bad for *this* Jew?" I ask.

"So selfish, Ruby. I'm embarrassed for the rabbi."

"Don't be," says Kevin graciously over my carcass. "I can take it."

My look is telling Essie Sue she'd better deliver the punch line fast.

"You promised to help with the matzo ball sale. Get it?"

"No."

"Matzo balls? Reduced fat? Interfaith Seder?"

"It's all coming together, Ruby, in one big extravaganza," Kevin says, obviously struggling to penetrate the density of my less enlightened brain.

Essie Sue's bursting. "The three of us are going to put on a Diet Interfaith Seder. My matzo balls and your wonderful organizational skills will be the pedestal upon which the rabbi will shine as conductor."

"Conductor? Orchestras? What?"

"Events this significant must be *conducted,* Ruby. You can't have people at the table reading willy-nilly with no guidance from above. Just look where that's gotten the Unitarians."

"Forget them. Why me?"

"That's a nonissue, Ruby. You've already promised to help with the matzo balls. Now the matzo balls are connected to something bigger, that's all."

"So is this sale just going to be a Passover thing?"

"No, of course not. Matzo ball soup is a year-round experience—we're selling these all year long, or at least as long as our customers want them. But the Seder connection is ideal. And remember our bargain—police information for your help with my project."

"Have you heard anything?"

"Maybe. I'll report to you this week if you'll go scout out a site for the Seder."

I guess I can be bought, and besides, we have a site.

"You're having it at the Temple, right?"

"No, I told you, Ruby, we think big now. This is community-wide—the Temple won't hold it. We're having it outdoors."

"Aren't you afraid of rain?" Silly question. I'm sure she's got the heavens doing her bidding, too.

"It's not going to rain. We're supposed to have a drought soon."

"Soon? Do you want to take that chance? It could pour."

"It wouldn't dare. Look at all the clergy we'll have."

I haven't heard lately that the Ministerial Council has added *Miraculous* to its title, but then again, they haven't come up against a force like this, either.

She changes the subject.

"Did I tell you what happened with the Diet Partner nominations from the other night's discussion at Temple? When you couldn't come to the decision meeting, we chose the winner without you. The runners-up will be contacted, too."

"I'm delighted."

"Don't you want to know who won?"

"I'm sure you're going to tell me."

"The last nomination: It was discussed and submitted in writing."

"Who wrote it?"

"I did—it's the Fit and Rural Reducing Ranch. These were the important people who had already received a tour of my Center a while back when they agreed to help process our matzo balls for us. They were terribly impressed with what I'd done. Rumor has it that movie stars from Hollywood are financing Fit and Rural."

"Don't you consider them competition?"

"No, I think our organizations complement one another. I'm a hometown exercise center par excellence, and they're an international residential fitness ranch. They're ready to promote me, and I'll promote them for anyone who wants to reduce in the country. They told me they have a huge patio area—they call it the Corral. We can have the Seder there."

"Have you seen the place?"

"Not yet. I've been wanting to go out there, but it's a ranch—so the roads are probably dusty. Maybe you can go look at it for me."

She looks around my kitchen as if to affirm her assumption that I'd enjoy a good roll in the mud.

"As a member of the committee, Ruby, you need to go, especially since we've contracted with them for the processing."

"What processing, again? Isn't this going to cost you plenty?"

"The Fit and Rural people have been picking up the large containers of matzo balls from the Center kitchen, and they're putting them into the six-packs we ordered. Then they're delivering them back here in dry ice for local pickup and nationwide shipping. You're well aware that we have a ridiculously small amount of counter space in the Center kitchen—we're stretching our facilities even to take care of the cooking."

"Just out of curiosity, how much for nationwide shipping?"

"You have some nerve to question my plans, since Milt turned me down flat when I asked to use the kitchen at The Hot Bagel, Ruby. Since the temple facility is small, too, I had no choice."

This means she spent plenty, but who's counting. I'm only thankful she didn't storm her way into the bakery.

Kevin's keeping his eyes down. I'm sure he'd like to keep the conversation away from the late Bogie's erstwhile employer.

I only have one more question, and then I plan to surprise her.

"So tell me, why did you have a contest about Diet Partners when you nominated the winner yourself, with no discussion?"

"I brought it up briefly before we adjourned, but you weren't listening. I believe in involving everyone, as you well know, without belaboring my own opinions. Congregants respond better in a democratic atmosphere. Besides, someone could have debated me at the meeting."

Yeah, just like the other Huns debated Attila. But we won't go there.

To Essie Sue's shock, she suddenly gets my complete cooperation.

"Okay, I'll check it out. But your police gossip had better be good."

"It's a deal."

This is an unexpected double whammy—I can obtain her information just by doing something I'd wanted an excuse to do anyway—get inside that guest ranch. Besides exploring the possibility of some computer work, I'm curious about what Kevin's told me about Bogie and the ranch.

She's ecstatic. "See, Rabbi—I told you I could handle Ruby. You don't have to be so scared of her. You could learn a few tricks from me."

What a lucky guy. With a teacher like this, who needs a seminary education?

"There is one more thing," she says to Kevin. This is her wheedling look—I've been the object of that before, and it's not a pretty sight. "I wanted to tell you in an atmosphere where I had Ruby's support."

Uh-oh. If she needs *my* support, this can't be good for Kevin. She stands up to deliver the missive, keeping her distance from the edge of my kitchen table. I think she's afraid her pale yellow linen spring suit might be contaminated by unknown crud she hasn't been able to wipe off with the three napkins she's used so far to sanitize her place setting.

"Rabbi, I know you're aware of the leadership responsibilities that come with your position as official conductor of the Seder. The whole ministry will be watching, along with their respective flocks, and we at the Temple want to be proud of you. Right, Ruby?"

"I'm not answering anything that might tend to incinerate me. I've been burned before."

"Then I'll go it alone."

He's in for it.

"This is, after all, Rabbi, a fitness occasion. I believe we're cutting new ground here with our joint idea of an Ecumenical Diet Seder."

No joint could save this idea, believe me.

"To put it bluntly, you must be more than a spiritual role model—you must be a physical role model as well. To the tune of twenty-five pounds."

Well, that's blunt enough, I guess. It hasn't sunk in yet—Kevin's still struggling to understand.

"Fitness, Rabbi. Fitness. You must be fit to lead in today's world. You've made a good start with your exercise program. I'm going to help you with your calories."

*Oy*—Little Red Riding Hood had better assistance from the Big Bad Wolf's grandmother act.

"Don't you think weight loss should be Kevin's decision?"

He looks up at me gratefully.

"I should have known that's the support I'd get from you, Ruby," Essie Sue says. "Your scale—"

"Don't even go there, Essie Sue, unless you want a knuckle sandwich." I have no idea where that came from, but I like it. Kevin does, too, though he's hiding his smile in the coffee cup.

She ignores my Cagney-ish threat. "We'll take it gently," she tells him.

We all know he's toast.

# 9

E-mail from: Ruby
To: Nan
Subject: *Homicide*

Well, it's official—the Bogie affair is now being ruled a homicide. Essie Sue found out that the investigation is accelerating. She's of course extremely disappointed that the matter is not just going to fade away, leaving the Center free to continue its bodily movements or whatever new craziness she cooks up. And I do mean cooks up. The whole gym is beginning to smell starchy. Believe me, that kitchen was never made to be the central cog in a matzo ball factory. She's got volunteers ladling matzo balls in foaming pots all over the place. If you've ever cooked matzo balls, you know how easily they can boil over, but these amateur cooks she's lassoed from all over town couldn't care less, as long as someone else is mopping up the floor.

Anyway, Essie Sue found out from one of her hangers-on at the gym that Lieutenant Lundy is now sure that the wound between Bogie's eyes was the cause of death, and that the fatality couldn't have been accidental. The angles don't support the theory that he fell and landed on a sharp object in the frontal position. Even if that were less certain, the autopsy gave no indication that anything had gone wrong internally to cause a fall. There was no sign of heart attack or stroke, and nothing toxic had been ingested or absorbed by other means.

The only baseballs found in the whole area were stacked inside the pitching machine. If a ball caused the injury, someone had to remove it, because it just *wasn't* there. If one of the batting tees or some other object caused the wound and was bloodied, where is it? And who would do such a thing, leaving the body behind, except the killer? Bogie's bat was lying on the ground, and it was clean, too.

More later.

E-mail from: Nan
To: Ruby
Subject: *Murder, Inc.?*

So are you going into the business or something? I can't believe another murder has turned up practically on your doorstep. Although I guess the real one I'd stay away from is Essie Sue—she must feel like the Angel of Death with her sister Marla dropping at her feet and now an employee killed in her own backyard.

Are you glad Lundy's on the case?

I feel as though I've been hit by a Mack truck this year, and I do so wish I could take the summer off. But I can't. First of all, it's smart to get an internship and start trying to connect with lawyers who hopefully will decide they can't do without me. And of course, even more important, I need the money. Trying to deal with all this and still pass my second semester courses is going to be a nightmare. But I do feel, finally, that I can survive this ordeal.

E-mail from: Ruby
To: Nan
Subject: *Law and Lawlessness*

It makes me feel good to hear you say you're going to survive—I haven't heard *that* from you all year. I had no doubt in my own mind, but of course, you know that already.

In answer to the teeny question you threw into the mix, I'm glad Lundy's on the case because I like him a lot, but I don't *like* him in the way I think you were asking. There's some chemistry, but no more than would fuel a very mild flirtation, trust me. Besides our more obvious differences, he's a workaholic and totally focused on rising in the ranks. I don't even want to know from the word *dedication* right now.

You?

I'll keep you posted on developments here.

And I'm proud of you!

# 10

The Fit and Rural Reducing Ranch, twenty miles from Eternal, doesn't quite live up to its name. It's not all that rural, and not much of a ranch, either. The place seems to be located in the middle of a cornfield—I guess that's the rural part, but just up the road is a sordid combination of feedlots, heavy equipment storage, and industrial encroachment.

Somehow the thought of an early morning fitness hike up to the spot where old tractors come to die doesn't exactly grab me—I hope the place has other attractions for its guests. I don't see any signs of a ranch—no horses or stables in sight unless I haven't noticed something, which I doubt because the land is too flat to miss much.

I drive up a straight road and run smack into my first hint of rurality—I don't think that's a word, but you get the picture. A weather-beaten gate has been imported from somewhere and bars my way, but not for long, since I steer around it. This makes no sense at all, but it seems the "ranch" is not fenced in—there's just the gateposts and the gate, bearing the wood-burned words WELCOME TO THE FIT AND RURAL REDUCING RANCH—WE TAKE IT OFF, YOU KEEP IT OFF, Y'ALL.

I get it—a little taste of Texas for non-Texans. Fair enough, although I'm surprised they added the bit ordering the clients to keep it off. After all, where's their repeat business going to come from?

As I approach the main complex, I see that all attempts at the rustic style have ended at the gate. From the outside, this place looks like a motel. Four rectangular buildings, two stories each with balconies, surround an oval swimming pool. As I get out of the car and start toward the only building with a portico, a matched set heads toward me. It's an older couple, short and squat, identically dressed in stiff jeans, red checkered shirts with denim vests, white Stetsons, and shiny red boots.

"Howdy," the man says in an accent that obviously hasn't howdied much, "welcome to Fit and Rural. We're the Poundburns. I'm Harmon; she's Hetty." Harmon's mouth is smiling, but his eyes are giving me the once-over.

"Why didn't you call us from the airport?" Hetty seems to be put out with me, or with whoever she thinks I am. "And where's your luggage?" My blue shorts, white tee shirt, and sandals seemed perfectly appropriate when I left home for what I thought would be spandex city, but they're not impressing the Poundburns.

"You're Mrs. Jerrold, right? From Pennsylvania?"

"No, I'm local—Ruby Rothman from Eternal—right up the road." Well, not exactly, but it might help explain the spur-of-the-moment drop-in. "I was driving out this way and thought I'd look in. You do take reservations from local clients, too, don't you?"

"Oh yes." Harmon's thawing a bit, but I can tell Hetty's having a hard time forgiving me for not calling from the airport.

"We got all dressed," she says. "We like our visitors to get a Texas welcome."

Out-of-town visitors, that is.

"I'm sure she'll be here soon," I soothe. I've never laid eyes on these people and am beginning to wish I hadn't, but that doesn't seem to stop me from wanting to make everything all right for them. Why do I do this? If I thought I'd left the excesses of Southern womanhood behind me, I realize I've got a long way to go.

"Do you want to book a stay?" Harmon's all business. Somehow I don't think this is the time to bring up my software application.

"No," I say—a tad uncomfortable standing in the middle of a cornfield in the presence of all this brand-new western ready-to-wear. I need to plunge in, though.

"I came on behalf of Mrs. Margolis at the Center for Bodily Movement in Eternal." I wouldn't be caught dead saying the Center's name in front of anyone capable of a snicker, but subtlety's a quality that has definitely left these two in the dust.

"Yeah, the lady we're packing the cartons for," Harmon says. "She sure is full of deals—wants us to do some promotions with her gym."

"That's the one." She didn't say she'd proposed any spectacular deals, but there's no mistaking that this time we've all got the right person. In some really sick way, I can just see them hitting it off.

"Do you think we could go inside? It's getting hot out here."

"I guess so," Hetty says. "We could talk to her in the lobby."

Graciousness personified. There's something familiar tugging at my memory, and I realize why. The Poundburns treat me just like Essie Sue does, and they don't even know me yet.

My view of the lobby only intensifies the sense of disconnectedness that hit me when I first saw this place. In contrast to its stark, concrete façade, Fit and Rural on the inside looks like the set from one of those evangelical cable TV shows starring big hair and big tears. Every inch is done in French Provincial—so brand spanking fresh you can smell the packing cartons. I haven't run into this much gilt since I read *Portnoy's Complaint*. They call this place a ranch?

Harmon and Hetty are not a pretty sight perched on a fragile sofa in their Roy Rogers and Dale Evans outfits—I can't figure out whether I'm supposed to think West Texas or western France. The place seems a bit empty of clientele, although I could be wrong—this *is* only the lobby. There's certainly no shortage of staff—they've fortunately been spared the western dress, and are rather comfortably running around in khaki shorts, white tee shirts with logos, and gym shoes.

"Do you suppose someone could bring me some water?" I'm dying of thirst, and there seems to be plenty of help around. But you'd think this was real chutzpah on my part—the Poundburns just stare at me.

"Okay, just point me toward the rest room," I say, "and I'll find some water on my own."

I'd like to see what's down the hall, anyway. I get up and head in the general direction of a doorway, and sure enough, they come to life just as I expected—they both jump up and run after me. I find this technique also works in restaurants when I can't get someone to bring my bill. I just head toward the exit and all hell breaks loose.

"There's a water fountain down the hall." Hetty finally catches up with me halfway down a long corridor that seems to be part of an administrative wing. Too bad for her—she's in clunky boots instead of gym shoes. I'm sure she won't let me out of her sight, so before she gets her bearings, I duck into one of the open doorways. As my mother-in-law used to say, *it vouldn't hurt*. This turns out to be an outer office complete with receptionist, adjacent to a massive mahogany door, which just happens to be ajar.

Two women are inside the room—a slight little thing is standing in front of a Louis XIV desk, in earnest conversation with the imposing woman behind it. I can see that I've startled them both.

"Oops, sorry," I manage to say, "I was looking for a water fountain."

The woman behind the desk, who has now risen, is wearing a black Chanel suit that says Fifth Avenue instead of Fifth Dimension, which is where I feel I've landed. High heels that couldn't cost less than three hundred dollars are clacking across the parquet floor toward me in my tee shirt and shorts. Hetty Poundburn, hair dripping with perspiration under her cowboy hat, has just stopped short in the doorway, while the fourth occupant of the room, looking like Laura Ashley courtesy of Singer sewing machine, with Birkenstocks, is staring at all of us.

Chanel suit finds her voice first.

"Are you a new client, dear?" She's trying to give me the once-over at the same time she's giving Hetty the eye.

Hetty takes the cue. "She's a friend of the Margolis woman."

Since nobody's introducing me, I introduce myself. "I'm Ruby Rothman from Eternal. And you are . . . ?"

Chanel suit starts to answer me, when Hetty interrupts.

"This is our social director here at Fit and Rural—Ardis Sommerfield. And this is our spiritual director, Angel Elkin."

Now it's my turn to be shocked. This is the first time Hetty's given any indication she's part of the civilized world. I have a feeling her introductions are not so much driven by good manners as they are an attempt at control. I can't figure out who's in charge here, but since Hetty's the manager, maybe she is. If I could get a look at *her* office, I guess I'd know.

"I also have a sideline," Ardis tells me. "I'm the president of Weddings Anonymous—I produce the ultimate in matrimonial extravaganzas."

Weddings Anonymous? *Oy*. "Do you know Essie Sue Margolis?" This just pops out of me—suddenly I'm imagining a supreme match of the misbegotten, and I doubt these two have already met. There's no way Essie Sue would have held back telling me about someone like Ardis.

"No, I've never had the pleasure. I have seen her gym a couple of times, though."

"Do you do any Jewish weddings? I'm surprised I never ran into you."

"Oh, we're all fairly new to the area—the whole crew of us. We're here to make Fit and Rural a success. And of course our clientele are the type who can obviously benefit from my bridal services, too."

Hetty's looking more and more uncomfortable. Her fit of manners must have taken a lot out of her. "We should be moving on," she says.

"To where?" I say. She's been so busy being hostile, she never really asked why I showed up here in the first place. I'm curious to see what she plans on doing with me.

"My husband's waiting for us."

"I'm Jewish," a voice pipes up. It's the spiritual director. I've never heard of that position at a fitness farm, but what do I know? One thing I do know—she'll have to fight to be heard in this crowd. So far, these people definitely seem on a par with Bogie. He was trying to be hired as athletic director, if I remember. And now Angel, the Jewish spiritual director.

"You should drop by our Temple sometime," I say by way of conversation.

"Oh, I don't think so. My own spirituality is certainly inclusive of my Jewish roots, but it's not where I'm at. It's like when the Universe calls, I don't want my line to be busy. You know?"

Probably, but I hope we never have to get into it. Angel is seriously intense in a way I find really, really boring. The only thing worse than a Valley Girl is a Valley Girl in search of meaning. I'm gonna get struck down for this.

"Do you have a database of client preferences?" I ask Ardis before Hetty can whisk me out of here. "I could help you with that. In fact, I recently put in an application here to design a computer system for your organization." I have an uncanny sense that my days are numbered on these premises once Harmon and Hetty have me to themselves again, and I want an excuse to come back. Maybe if I have witnesses for this software job, the Poundburns won't be able to ignore it.

"Oh, I think computers are terribly important," Ardis tells me. "Have you spoken to our public relations director, Sonny Maples? He's in charge of business applications."

I make a mental note of Sonny.

"Do you know about Nirvana Net: A Site to Behold? You have to drop by this site for a real treat," Angel says. Apparently, they're all wired here. Except maybe Hetty, who's still pulling my arm.

She's no dummy, though, and has already picked up on the teensy inconsistencies in my presentation.

"I thought you said you came here on behalf of Mrs. Margolis," she says after she finally drags me out of there. "Now you say you've applied for a position here. Which is it?"

I never meant to blurt out the part about the software, but now I'm stuck with it. Besides, I'm glad in a way that I got my foot in the door with Ardis and Angel.

"Well, a little of both. I didn't apply for a position, by the way—your notice in the newspaper solicited a professional consultant." My pride has engendered this distinction, which she couldn't care less about, I'm sure. But I can't deal with her thinking I might want to join the panoply of stars here as the director of databases.

"I'm also on Mrs. Margolis's fund-raising committee, and she's interested in exploring the possibility of using your facilities for a community-wide Passover Seder ceremony, since you're already working together in processing her matzo balls. The Seder would bring lots of people to the ranch from Eternal. Perhaps you'd like me to speak to the public relations director—maybe I made a mistake in making this request on such a high level. I'm sure, as the manager, you have a system for delegating these issues."

I'm in high shoveling-it-on mode now, so I might as well keep going. Essie Sue would *plotz,* since she always goes to the top, but she also wouldn't be beneath a little flattery if necessary.

My instincts are right, and Hetty immediately softens.

"This is the right place to start," she says. "My husband and I like to do things from the top down, not the opposite. That way, we know what's going on around here and don't have any surprises. All our employees like Ardis, Angel, and Sonny know that we don't like surprises."

Well, she's put them in their place.

"Should we talk in your office?" I wanna see what the top looks like here.

"That won't be necessary."

Okay, she's put me in my place, too. Now what?

I don't find out because Harmon appears and leads us to yet another corridor.

"I do hope I can see the facilities," I throw in.

"Yep, that's where we're headed," he says.

"You'd better guide her through," Hetty tells him. "She has a tendency to wander."

# 11

We see a few scattered guests in the exercise room, but there are still more staff than clients, or whatever you call them. I think I'm supposed to be checking on the picnic facilities for the outdoor Seder that should never happen, but they're now treating me as a potential customer. Yeah, to the Poundburns, *customer* definitely sounds better than *client*. And then there's the software connection, so I've got a three-pronged attack going here. If I've got such great ammunition, I wonder why I'm already feeling outgunned.

So far, the place looks like Essie Sue's gym—the weights, the stairs, the treadmills. As we peek into the dining room with the crystal chandelier, though, I'm beginning to see more signs of the alleged movie star connection. Somebody has poured a lot of money into this guest ranch. The mirrored aerobics rooms are no slouch, either, and I even get a tour of a model guest room in the third wing. It's king-sized, and looks like Essie Sue's boudoir, except the closet's not so big.

Harmon can see I'm impressed, though I'm trying not to give him the satisfaction.

"Wanna see the kitchen where we're packing your friend's matzo balls?" Such an appealing guy.

"Sure, Mr. Poundburn, but first, just tell me where the rest room is."

"Hetty, go with her."

Hetty's a shoo-in for the role of warden, and I'm dead certain she's planning on standing outside my toilet stall with folded arms. We start down the corridor, but this time, she walks ahead of me, so I'm trapped. We enter the single rest room door double-file like a couple of Keystone Kops. Aha—Angel's in here, too. I greet her like an old friend—anybody's better than going lockstep with Hetty.

"Angel, since you're spiritual director"—I'm having trouble spitting out that title with a straight face—"do you think we could confer on the site for our Seder? I'm sure those arrangements will be part of your responsibility."

"Of course, Mrs. Rothman."

She turns to my captor. "Hetty, I'll be glad to show her our outdoor facilities."

"Oh, great," I say. "And call me Ruby." We walk out

arm in arm, with Hetty right behind us, looking around for Harmon.

"We have a beautiful covered patio area that can seat a couple of hundred people by the pool," Angel tells me. "I remember Seders from my childhood, and I can't wait to help with the planning for this one. Will a rabbi be taking part?"

"Oh yes." I consider embarking on a conversational description of Kevin, but frankly, I'm not up to it. She'll meet him soon enough. I switch the subject to Essie Sue.

"Have you met Mrs. Margolis?"

"No, she's made all her arrangements for the matzo ball sales with our managers. A few of the staff have visited the Center for Bodily Movement, but I haven't had the pleasure yet."

*Oy*. We'll see if she's still into the pleasure principle after a few planning sessions with Essie Sue. I keep up the chatter, though—Hetty seems to have gone after Harmon.

"I think Mrs. Margolis is planning an ecumenical Seder, Angel. We'll have guests of all faiths here."

I've struck the right chord. Angel is absolutely glowing—she even puts her hands out together in angelic fashion.

"This is a dream come true, Ruby. Religious parochialism has always upset me terribly. Why can't we all embrace one another under the great umbrella of spirituality? The Seder, especially, is such a universal occasion."

Yes and no. I have my own unscholarly bone to pick on that subject, but Angel wouldn't want to hear it. No question that model Seders are sprouting up all over the place these days—the Passover theme of freedom from slavery is definitely universal, and yep, the stranger in our midst is certainly welcomed with open arms.

But I can't think of a more in-group occasion myself. This *is* the night, after all, when we recount the boils of our enemies, promise next year in Jerusalem, and re-create the tears and mortar from those sentimental old days when we were plastering bricks for the Pharaoh. A rough history, but it's ours, and we're still here—toasting with Manischewitz. I guess the Manischewitz will have to go at the Ecumenical Diet Seder—too many calories.

"It'll be an interesting experience for you to work with the rabbi and Mrs. Margolis, Angel."

"I can't wait, Ruby. I know I'll learn a lot from them."

More than you'll ever want to know, honey. I try to steer Angel off the patio for her own tour of the kitchen area, but it's not to be. Harmon shows up, almost on cue. Apparently, he and Hetty have been keeping an eye on us.

"Let's do that kitchen now, so you can tell Mrs. Margolis you saw it, and then you can be on your way."

I don't think these guys appreciate my creative touring. Well, next time they can host Essie Sue and Kevin. I'm sure she'll drive out here, now that she's had me explore the alien territory alone. We all know I'm expendable. I'm disappointed that I didn't have a chance to bring up Bogie's name or his death or whatever, but my instincts tell me another time.

We head toward the pièce de résistance—a large, modern kitchen that would make a French chef jealous. I'm still reeling over the budget it must have taken to build and furnish this health spa. Two tall women and a man, all wearing chef's hats, are chopping vegetables. Angel's tagged along with us, and converses with each of them—a nice touch, considering the imperiousness of the managers, who speak to no one. Including me.

Through a glass partition, I can see some sort of refrigerator room adjoining the kitchen. Harmon walks in there, motioning for me to follow. It's a refrigerated room—he calls it a *cold room,* and it's the antechamber to an enormous walk-in freezer. From the cold room you can see the contents of the freezer through very thick glass windows. Harmon opens the freezer door and I feel transported to one of the poles—now *this* is where I'd like to spend my Texas summers. I don't choose to go in, but I see boxes and boxes of matzo ball cartons all lined up on shelves. Fit and Rural seems to have done a good processing job—I'd still love to know how much they were paid for it, but I don't expect to get anything out of the Sphinx here. Maybe if I get the software contract, I can find out.

Which reminds me. As we leave the kitchen area and go back through the lobby to the parking lot, I put in another plug for the job.

"I could install that database you need in less time than you might think," I tell Harmon. And since Essie Sue owes me one for having just spent three hours here, I add her name as a reference.

"I work with Mrs. Margolis quite a bit—she can vouch for me."

"Hiring a consultant—that's another department," Harmon says.

Like hell it is. One thing I've learned today—the little dictator in chaps has his hands in everything, *including* the matzo balls.

# 12

Bradley Axelrod, who's now our second-in-command at the bakery, has just brought over a piping hot basket of rye bagels. Kevin and our guest of the afternoon, Angel Elkin, dive in with gusto. Essie Sue passes, but Milt and I reach for ours with such enthusiasm you'd never suspect we handle the production of hundreds of these every day. This fact hasn't escaped Essie Sue.

"I can't believe you two can stand to look at another bagel," she says, moving the basket away from Kevin and depositing it in front of Milt. She doesn't care if Milt drops dead from a carbo overdose or not.

"The coffee's good." This is directed at me—rare praise indeed.

"I didn't think there was anything this fabulous outside L.A.," Angel puts in. Angel's from Half Moon Bay near San Francisco, but for some reason I can't yet fathom, the City of Angels is her measuring rod for all that's true and beautiful. "It's the Jewish Mecca," she assures us, ignoring New York and south Florida. "A corned beef sandwich in L.A. is unmatched anywhere else." Anyone who's ever visited New York's Carnegie or Wolfie's might disagree, but we don't argue. We're happy she's here.

Essie Sue and I, in an unprecedented show of unity, have invited Angel to help plan the Ecumenical Diet Seder. Essie Sue's happy because Angel seems to genuinely support every bizarre idea she comes up with, and I'm happy to pluck Angel out of the Poundburns' orbit long enough to try to get more information. Essie Sue has just appointed Kevin and Angel cochairs of the Seder. Better her than me for a change, and Angel seems ready for the challenge. I realize that's because she doesn't know what's in store for her, but I'll bet she's also glad to get away from Fit and Rural for a few hours.

We've hashed over Seder plans, and now Angel and Kevin are debating the merits of "softening" Judaism's image. Kevin's against it.

"Guilt keeps us in line, Angel. We need a good dose of reality. You should hear me preach about this sometime." He's getting excited, and taking big bites of his bagel while he's talking. Probably afraid it's going to be taken away from him anytime now.

"Why do we have to turn such a harsh face to the world, Rabbi? From lemons we should make rainbows. And what's all this standing up and sitting down we have to do in services? Bor—ing. Instead, if we stuck our hands in challah dough together more often, we could learn from it. Now *that* would be a Shabbat experience. The smells, the sounds, the feel of the flour and water—that's what Jewish memories are made of. We need more hands-on activities."

We're talking apples and oranges here, but what else is new. "Let's get into something else for a minute," I say.

"You're interrupting a significant debate, Ruby. I, for one, am learning something." Essie Sue puts the bagel basket on an adjacent table, ignoring Milt's glare as he gets up to leave, and pins me down. "You're always pushing your own agenda. Listen and learn."

This from the woman who put the *push* in *pushy,* but I wait my turn. At least until the debate heats up over whether the High Holy Days should be permanently moved up to cooler weather. Then I excuse myself and go over to look at the day's receipts. I figure even Essie Sue won't last much longer, and she doesn't. When this woman says listen and learn, she's not including herself. I know Kevin has to drive her home, so I grab the chance to go speak to Angel.

"I have some very appealing hands-on Judaica at home, Angel. If you don't have to go back yet, can you come over for a while?"

She's interested, and when Kevin and Essie Sue leave, I give Angel directions to my house.

The first thing she says when she arrrives is, "So where's the hands-on Judaica?"

I have to think fast, since I made that up. I lead her to the spice box—filled with aromatic spices—ensuring a sweet Sabbath, and point out how it appeals to the sense of smell. Before she asks me to produce more, I give her a comfortable chair, some iced tea, and ask a few questions.

"Do you like working at Fit and Rural, Angel?"

"Of course. Why wouldn't I?" She's immediately wary. I could blow this if I'm not careful.

"Just making conversation. Do the owners live in L.A.? We hear they're going after the movie star crowd."

"Oh yes, it'll be very glamorous once we have a full house. I think it's glamorous already, don't you?"

"Well, it's certainly expensively furnished. Did Ardis oversee the decorating, or did the Poundburns do it?"

"What makes you think Ardis did it?"

"Her office is so fashionable, I thought maybe the place reflected her taste."

"I really can't say what part Ardis or the Poundburns had in the decorating. I think a decorator was sent in by the owners when the ranch was built."

"The Poundburns run the show on this end?"

"I guess you could say so."

I'm getting nowhere here, so I switch subjects.

"Angel, did you know a man who went by the name of Bogie? I think he was interested in the job of athletic director."

She's pale now. "He's dead. I read about it in the paper."

"Yes, that was terrible. The police have been all over the gym. Poor Essie Sue."

"I . . . I don't want to discuss this."

"Sure. I didn't mean to upset you. I was just wondering if they'd been asking questions there, too. Since he might have been doing some work there."

"You said he was interested in a job, not that he worked at our place."

She's got me there—I can't say Kevin told me. But I'm shocked that she seems so nervous.

"I guess it'll all come out when the police finish their investigation," I say. "I hear they think he was murdered."

Angel reaches for her purse, knocking over the iced tea in the process.

"Don't worry—Oy Vay'll take care of it," I joke.

She doesn't smile. "I have to be going now, Ruby. Thanks for the invitation."

It's obvious she's trying to pull herself together. "I really enjoyed meeting Essie Sue and the rabbi. You've all been very nice."

"I'll look forward to seeing you again, Angel. I'm on your committee."

I almost ask her to put in a good word for me re the software job, but I decide I'm further in the hole now than I was when I visited the ranch. I think I need a PR director of my own.

# 13

E-mail from: Ruby
To: Nan
Subject: *Feedback After the Fact*

I'm asking your advice on something I've already done—but what else is new? I really haven't been certain how to insinuate myself into the infamous fat farm family I wrote you about. I need to find out what those people know about Bogie. He had two professional connections—maybe related, maybe not. We know a lot about his work as a trainer for Essie Sue's gym, and less about his interest in being athletic director at Fit and Rural.

Essie Sue's latest information dovetails with what Paul Lundy's told me about the police investigation of her gym—the leads aren't going anywhere. The cops have talked to everyone around—staff and members alike—and no threads to the murder have developed yet. Since nothing's happening, I think I owe it to myself to poke around the ranch. Angel's drop-dead reaction to my mention of Bogie, together with the general Poundburn paranoia, have me wondering what, if anything, is going on out there.

After the lukewarm welcome I got when I made my first drop-in visit, I thought the best way to explore the place might be in my official capacity as a member of the Ecumenical Diet Seder committee. But how many visits can you make to count the folding chairs? Kevin, on the other hand, gets to go out there plenty to plan the Seder service. Since his cochairman, Angel, is such a flake, she's not a good bet to orient the staff as to just what the holiday entails, what the Seder symbols are, etc., so Essie Sue's depending on him to fill in the gap. In other words, he has a purpose there that I don't. Essie Sue went with him a couple of times—and, as I had thought, she was mightily impressed. She'd already met the Poundburns when they came to the Center for the original matzo ball production meeting, so when it was their turn to play host, they went all out for her visit, western regalia and all.

Essie Sue, like Angel, thought Ardis was a bit too aggressive—ha, that's because they're so much alike—and raved about the public relations director, Sonny Maples. He gave her the full treatment, obviously. I knew she'd take to the high-priced decor at the ranch, but she was disappointed she didn't see any celebrities.

Anyway, all the fuss they make about Essie Sue and Kevin still leaves me out in the cold, so I had to rethink my software application. I persuaded Essie Sue that this would give me an excuse to hang out at the ranch and oversee the Seder preparations. Since I don't think she trusts Kevin *or* Angel to organize the event properly, and doesn't want to have to schlep out there herself on dusty roads all the time, she figures I'll be her best bet. She set up an interview for me with Sonny tomorrow. He's the only one of the management crew I haven't met yet, so it should be interesting, and needless to say, I'll be on my best behavior.

Do you think the software route was the best way to go? I figure it'll net me a few bucks besides.

E-mail from: Nan
To: Ruby
Subject: *Why Not?*

Yeah, I think you did the right thing going for the database job. At least it'll keep you earning while you snoop—something you don't always manage, Rubeleh. Too bad it's Passover time—you could sell 'em bagels while you're at it! Maybe later, huh?

And while you're looking, don't you think it's strange that no expense has been spared in a place that has so few clients? I mean, all that staff and all those fancy interiors in a place that looks like a 1930s shoot-'em-up movie set on the outside? I think it's weird.

# 14

As I park in front of Fit and Rural's main entrance, I half expect to see the welcoming committee in twin Stetsons heading toward me, but I'm apparently going to be spared that Poundburn Moment for the time being. Oh goodie—maybe I can walk in unnoticed and go looking for the Public Relations office on my own, with a few stops on the side.

No such luck. There's a very efficient young lady at the registration desk, and she's having none of my wanderlust. She calls me back from the corridor and makes me give her Sonny's name like a regular person, even though I offer to go find him. While we're waiting for him to answer her page, I ask how long she's been working here.

"Ever since we opened," she tells me, "and before that when we were getting settled."

"Do they pay well? I'm here about some work myself." I figure this isn't too intrusive for a fellow toiler in the vineyard, but she ignores it. Who trained these people anyway? Whatever happened to the loose lips I'm used to in every other walk of life these days?

Sonny doesn't keep me waiting. He looks like Rock Hudson in better days, although Rock in those early movies also came across as the Rock of Gibraltar, which is not a name you'd use to describe Sonny, unless you're talking slippery slope. Sonny is smooth. He slips an arm around my shoulders before a word comes out of his mouth, and I'm caught between my natural impulse to shrug it off before you can say Oval Office, and my less admirable side, which is urging me to wimp out for now and reap great rewards with the personnel files when I get hired.

I wimp out, and don't even think badly of myself for it, which only goes to show how far I've come since catching killers became part of my résumé. Well, I've actually only caught one so far, but I'm not passing up any opportunities.

"Ruby, I'm Sonny." He turns to shake my hand in one of those deals where the one-on-one handshake becomes his two hands massaging my one. He's now said exactly three words to me while rubbing me the wrong way twice. Oh yes, I'm counting.

"Nice to know you, Sonny." Not. But I'm on my own slippery slope now. I use the maligned hand to point toward the offices, so he has to let it go—either that or dance with me.

"You were the only one I missed meeting last time I was here," I say in high-cordial mode. "Harmon said you took care of all the hiring for Fit and Rural."

Sonny's sculpted square jaw drops at that one, but he makes a fast recovery.

"Oh yes, I have lots of responsibilities. We have quite a large staff if you've noticed. Why don't you come into my office and we'll talk?"

I'll bet *that's* a well-used line. But since mine's not to reason why, I meekly follow him into the administrative suite. This time, though, nobody seems to be around. He leads me into an office that's as large as Ardis's was, but a lot less shiny. This one's done in tones of brown and tan—I can live with this. Uh-oh. I notice there's no desk at all—a mahogany worktable in the corner, two—count 'em—two long sofas where the desk ought to be, and one leather chair and ottoman.

I run for the chair, thanking my lucky stars that I learned to size up a room fast in my bar mitzvah dinner days. Dinner was usually served at nine, and the cocktail party started at seven. Like musical chairs, anyone unwary enough to be caught on her feet when all the chairs were taken was stuck making cocktail conversation for two hours in high heels; not a pretty fate. I could case a room faster than it took to order a martini with a twist.

I think Sonny's used to having applicants run for the chair. In an obviously well-rehearsed move, he slides onto the ottoman before I can put my feet up. This is more intimate than sitting beside him on the sofa would be—he's practically in my lap. My move—I take my big old leather pouch purse from the floor and stick it between us. Since it weighs as much as a two-year-old, it's very effective, giving me distance to jump up and admire the photos on the wall. This is not gonna be a cinch. And it's living proof of how much good it does to wimp out.

"Is this your, uh, family?" I'm looking at a photo of three babes surrounding a much younger Sonny. Who knows—they could be his sisters. Since I've stuck myself smack in front of this one, I have to say *something* about it as an excuse for jumping up.

"Those are Hollywood starlets. I represented all of 'em in those days. I can still do a lot for a pretty girl." He's leering, yet. Why couldn't I have stood in front of some old army buddies?

"Harmon told me you were in charge of having the client and staff databases computerized. I can quote you an hourly fee if you're interested. He wanted me to let him know when we'd had our appointment, but I'd like to look at your present system first."

I head out the door before it's locked on me, and Sonny follows. Looking like I know where I'm going, I turn down the hall toward some open doors.

"Hey, let up. We weren't through with our appointment." Yeah, we're through with it—he just doesn't know it yet.

"I thought the file room was down here," I say over my shoulder. "I remember from my last visit."

"Well, you remembered wrong. They're in the basement."

No way am I going down to the basement with this guy. But if I do get this job, having the files in the basement will be a real plus—I won't have to look over my shoulder every five minutes.

I'm talking loud enough to attract *someone,* I hope. Where's that big staff when I need them?

I'd love to avoid Harmon and Hetty, and I have a feeling they'd have made an appearance by now if they were around. But I'll take anyone else, and I do mean anyone.

I hear the click of heels. Hallelujah. It's Ardis, rounding the corner and running right into me.

"Mrs. Rothman—I didn't see you coming."

"Please call me Ruby." I mean that—she's now my new best friend. Maybe the three of us can get this job pinned down, now that I'm out of Dodge City.

"Essie Sue Margolis told me how much she enjoyed meeting you," I tell her. "She told me she could give me her highest reference—I set up her computer system at the Center. Since Sonny's in charge of all this, I was just ready to gather some information from him so that I could make a fair bid."

"Do we need to take a meeting?" Ardis addresses this question to Sonny, but it's obvious she doesn't want to hear *yes* for an answer. She's halfway to her office already, flicking me a good-bye as she goes.

"No," Sonny yells. He's suddenly totally uninterested in meetings, bids, or trips to the basement. I'm tickled, but I keep appropriately serious.

"Harmon says you can do most of this from home, since we don't have a lot of office space," Sonny says.

They have nothing but space, but I couldn't care less. All I need is some time alone in the basement.

"If I can look down there to see how big the job is, I can have the quote on your desk immediately. It'll be comparable to other software services in the area."

"I'm sure your bid will be fine," he says, and I know I'm in, even before I give the quote. I guess they're treating Essie Sue with kid gloves. I'm certain Sonny knew he was going to hire me from the beginning—he just wanted a little action from the grateful bidder.

"Just point me to the basement stairs."

"Not today—you can come back tomorrow. I'm ready to go for the day, and I want to go down there with you."

"But it'll only take a little while to see the scope of the work, and I honestly think I can do just fine by myself."

"Nope. Tomorrow."

He's all business now, and I can see he means it. I don't think this is the time to push, but I sure don't want him hovering when I do my work. Not to mention other basement activities he might consider part of the job description.

He walks me out of the building, so I couldn't see anything even if I wanted to.

As I'm driving off in my car, I see another car parked between the trees right next to the fenceless wood-burned gate. I don't know the car and it's not facing my way, but a woman is sitting in the driver's seat with a man next to her. Their heads are together.

If I didn't know better, I'd swear it was Kevin and Angel.

# 15

It's a good thing this is a country road—my driving's a bit erratic. I'm sure I must have been mistaken about seeing Kevin—his car wasn't in the ranch parking lot, and he barely knows Angel. Nevertheless, that was such an odd scene—heads together like teenagers seeing a movie. Or at any rate, the way teenagers used to see movies—who knows now? My own son says I'm in a time warp.

As if my concentration weren't bad enough, the cell phone rings. I hate answering these things while I'm driving, but of course, I do it. I can't believe the rest of America is so well coordinated that it doesn't feel the same sense of disorientation I do. Frankly, I'm surprised the accident rates haven't snowballed since these things came out.

It's Paul Lundy from the police station.

"Ruby? I need to bounce a few things off you. Can you come down now?"

Paul's a favorite of mine, but he annoys me sometimes. Maybe it's just the authoritarian imperative that comes with the territory, or the fact that he speaks in shorthand—at any rate, I always feel he pulls out the hoop whenever he feels like it and I'm supposed to jump through it. Like now—it's "Can you come down now?" not "I'd like you to come down," or "Let's figure out a convenient time for you to come down," or "I realize you have a life, Ruby." After all, I'm not a suspect. If this were Milt's personality, we'd never be in partnership—that's for sure.

So of course I jump through the hoop and I'm at the station in twenty minutes. I also remember that just a short time ago I was dying for an excuse to find out what's going on with his investigation. But still.

"You can at least send out for a decent cup of coffee, Lundy. And how about something to go with it? I was headed home for dinner."

"A candy bar, or peanut butter crackers?"

I guess this is as close to an apology as I'm going to get.

We're on either side of a long table in the interrogation room—very apt.

"I want to see if I can tie some of these threads together, Ruby, and since you know most of the players, I thought maybe I could run things by you again. Hubert Bogardis was—"

"Who?"

"Hubert Bogardis—the victim. That's his name."

I'd forgotten—that explains a lot. I'd rather be Mr. Muscle, too, than go around the school yard with that name. Of course, the *real* Bogie's name wasn't the essence of macho, either, I recall.

I suddenly realize I was going to look for Bogie's personnel file tomorrow without even remembering his full name from the newspaper accounts—that would have been intelligent. I make a mental note without saying anything to Paul yet about the files. I don't want to be told to keep my nose out of this.

"I was trying to tell you something, Ruby." I guess I can be annoying, too. I pay attention.

"The victim was found on his back. Since none of the possible weapons were found with bloodstains on them, I told you I had suspected that one of his practice balls had killed him. That could still be the case, except that no balls were found near the body—or anywhere except neatly stacked in the machine. Why would the killer go to the trouble of setting up the batting machine to aim at Bogie's head as if it were an accident, and then remove the ball?

"We think now that Bogie was just setting up his practice session when he was killed. Since it was such a helluva night out there—blustery and cold—no one was out there except the victim, and then the killer. I think Bogie was taken by surprise and might not even have made a sound. He was probably out there dead for a couple of hours before you found him."

"The rabbi found him, too—not just me."

"I interviewed Rabbi Kapstein twice. The last time, he told me that Bogardis had wanted to change jobs, but didn't want Mrs. Margolis to find out. We went out to the guest ranch he told us about, and interviewed the managers. Their reaction was odd."

"That's because they *are* odd. You interviewed Harmon and Hetty Poundburn, right?"

"Yeah. At first, they looked blank—as if they didn't know him, but they didn't actually say they didn't know him—they just waited for more questions. You know—cooperative but not cooperating. We get that a lot. Anyway, they said he was interested in the position of athletic director out there, but we got the idea from some employees lower on the ladder that he was already acting as athletic director on a lesser salary. The Poundburns hedged and said he had an association with them and hung around a lot."

"Which could be true, Paul. He might have had some agreement with Essie Sue he was trying to get around. Did you ask her?"

"We didn't know this when we interviewed her. The rabbi only told us in his second interview, and he said you encouraged him to tell us. That's how I figured you were up to your ears in this already."

We both ignore this remark.

"Right now we're in the middle of going through all Mrs. Margolis's employment records, and I want to hold off on another interview with her until I've reviewed everything. We're also looking at the guest ranch records."

"Uh—my bid was just accepted for a job out there designing a database for them. Believe it or not, I applied for that job months ago from an ad in the paper."

"And you thought the employment records might just be lying around unsecured after all this, and you could get a look?"

"Well, I didn't know for sure. I had no idea how far the investigation had progressed, and I figured it couldn't hurt."

"Your motto, if I remember."

"Okay, maybe I won't find anything in the files, but I do have the job. I was going to suggest to you that I could keep my eyes open and maybe I could pick up something."

"That's fine. Keep me informed. But let's get back to the rabbi. Do you think he could be keeping something back from us? He knew the guy better than anyone, or so he says. And yet he didn't come forward with the lowdown about Bogardis's job out there the first time he talked to us. I wonder what else he's holding back?"

"Surely you're not thinking of him as a suspect?"

"I'm not ruling him out, although you're right—he's not someone I'd gravitate to for that purpose. But he could be a good source of information, and I don't feel we're getting that. Think about it. He was close enough to the guy to have Bogardis confide in him about wanting that job—even when Bogardis knew the rabbi was friendly with Mrs. Margolis. That says to me they were pretty close."

Now's my chance to mention what I thought I saw in the car parked at the ranch, but I can't do it. First of all, I'm not sure I really recognized either of them—it wouldn't be fair to bring it up without checking it out. How I'm going to check it out is a problem.

I can tell him about having Angel at my house, though, and I try to explain how she froze up when I asked about Bogie. I definitely get his attention.

"Angel, huh? That's very interesting, Ruby. I hadn't paid much attention to her—she's not one of those people who sings out to you in a crowd, you know?"

"I do know—she stays in the background. But I'll bet anything she had some knowledge of Bogie. Either that, or someone else at the ranch did, and she's afraid to discuss it."

I've now dunked and eaten all the crackers on the paper plate, and I'm still hungry for dinner. But now that I'm here, I don't want to cut this short if there's anything else I can find out from Paul.

"Sounds to me as if you've got to find a way to open some mouths, Paul."

"You can say that again. I've gotta spend more time out at that ranch—and yeah, now that I think of it, your job there could be useful to us. They let us look at the papers already—I saw the Bogardis file and a few others. But see if you can get friendly with some of them."

"Trust me—you don't *get* friendly with Hetty and Harmon—I'd have more luck with a pair of lox. Or is it a pair of loxes? But I *can* get closer to Ardis, and maybe even to Angel, if I don't come at her directly next time. I know I was a little bit heavy-handed."

I get a grin out of him. "That's a failing we both share, Ruby."

"How about the PR guy—Sonny? I think he's ready to keep his hands off me after our last encounter, so maybe we can talk. I can tell he's a schmoozer." I tell him about Sonny's classic study of how not to conduct a job interview.

"You'd go at it after he did that?"

"Oh, sure. I handled him before, and I can do it again."

"Just watch it, kid."

"Yeah, yeah. I've got an even better chance to work with all these people at the Seder Essie Sue's planning out there. And you know all about the matzo ball sale they're helping her with."

"Oh, sure. We took the whole Center kitchen apart as a part of the murder scene investigation. I was up to my ass in matzo balls."

Paul gives me a glance I've come to know in my association with him as the *Should I, shouldn't I?* look. Fortunately, I'm able to hide my own version of that look from *him*—otherwise, I'd have had less success in holding back that bit about possibly seeing Kevin and Angel. But when Paul does it, it's a dead giveaway.

"So what were you going to tell me before I leave?"

"How do you know I was going to tell you anything?"

"Come on—I'm starving, and so is Oy Vay. She's probably tearing up my yard as we speak."

"Okay. I haven't said anything to anyone outside the office about this, because I don't really know what to make of it, if anything. So keep your mouth shut."

"I promise. Especially when you ask in such a charming manner."

"Remember when I said there wasn't much to go on in the area where we found Bogie's body? Well, there was something peculiar we discovered in the guy's pants pocket. It was a melted lump of meal."

"You mean a matzo ball? He had one of Essie Sue's matzo balls in his pocket?"

# 16

I'm back in the saddle again—my old hoss of a car can almost lope up to the ranch on automatic pilot now. Which is a good thing, because I'm on automatic pilot myself. I was wired all night thinking about the matzo ball in Bogie's pocket, and I don't think I slept more than two or three hours. Not that all the thinking did me any good. Maybe the machine batted a frozen matzo ball at him and the evidence melted like the leg of lamb in that old Hitchcock thriller. Yeah, sure—and then the remains of the matzo ball went right through to his pocket by osmosis?

Forget that—I have work to do today. And my first task is to figure out how to do my basement job without the supervision of my supervisor. I cross the lobby and head for the stairway, but three staff members appear from nowhere to smile me into submission.

"We'll call Mr. Maples," the receptionist tells me as I stand in front of the blocked stairway. What do they think this place is—the Pentagon?

"Mr. Maples doesn't seem to be in. Do you have an appointment?"

"No, I work here. I'm working on the basement personnel files to produce a client and staff database. Why don't I wait down there for him? Either way, the ranch is being charged for my time. I don't think he'd appreciate it if you just let me sit here racking up hours, do you?" I try to make my expression sweeter than that question sounds, since I'm sending a double message here—self-assured but nice employee doesn't want to waste a moment.

"The management staff's in a meeting right now," the receptionist tells me. "I guess you might as well get started and I can let them know you're here when the meeting is over. They asked not to be disturbed." She doesn't sound all that sure of herself, so I try to sound confident enough for both of us.

"Do you want to quickly pull someone out of the meeting? I'm sure they won't mind your interruption." She nods a definite *no,* and I'm allowed to pass down the stairs.

As Paul Lundy reminded me, what's in the basement has either been found by the police already or has been shredded by the management, so I'm not expecting any breakthroughs. Still, it would be nice if the meeting lasted long enough for me to get into the job. I just didn't like the idea of Sonny breathing down my neck today. In more ways than one.

This area has a new-basement smell to it—not that I can ever remember being in a new basement—but I'm sure this is what one should smell like. Shellac and drywall predominate, with a little glue tone here and there. My first thought is that I'm glad I have other work. From these files, I wouldn't want to make a living. The phrase "files in the basement" conjures up a musty history, and it just hits me that this place doesn't *have* a history—nor does it have many files in the basement.

The only dust here seems to be sawdust, which is all over the big worktable I'm commandeering as my desk. The file cabinets and folders are all brand spanking new, and whoever was in charge of producing these personnel documents didn't suffer from overwork. I know skimpy when I see it.

I plunge into the staff files, but if I'm lucky, I can get an overview of the client files, too, before the Poundburns come running down here. As I thought, the training staff isn't being overpaid—but then, with résumés featuring such highlights as assistant cashier of Sports Department at Wal-Mart, maybe the ranch represents a promotion after all.

Bogie's file is still here, but it's much less detailed than the one Essie Sue showed me from the Center. Of course, it *would* be if he only worked here unofficially. No—he was on salary as an athletic assistant—I guess he was moonlighting. Not much here, though. Born in '69. After high school in Lubbock, he worked in El Paso for nine years, from 1987 to 1996. I guess those were the Mr. Texas Muscle years.

I flip through the senior staff information. Ardis is from Chicago, where she was also a wedding consultant. Wonder why she came here? She doesn't seem particularly fit or rural to me. I keep having to remind myself that this place is outfitted for celebrities—even though there aren't any. Or at least they're nonvisible to me so far. Maybe Ardis could see the possibilities.

Angel Elkin's file says she's from Half Moon Bay, California—knew that. Before she came here, she lived in L.A. for two years—suspected that. That's all on the application, including junior college, from '86 to '88. But there's also a long, essay-type letter in here, where she's making a pitch for the job in her usual, loquacious style.

*Dear Mr. and Mrs. Poundburn,*

*This is a follow-up letter to our wonderful conversation in Los Angeles. I would be deeply honored if you were to see your way clear to appoint me to the position of spiritual director of what I know will be the premier health spa from the West Coast to the Mississippi, and beyond.*

*Though my spirituality has been shaped by all that the California coast has to offer in the way of sophistication, cutting-edge universality, and the deep resonance of the Pacific Ocean, I also want to remind you of my more mid-American roots. The eight years I spent in El Paso, Texas, after college were central to the formation of my character. The mountains and valleys deep in the heart of the blue skies of West Texas taught me that the Earth could compete with the more watery elements to form a more perfect union in our land . . .*

I'm nodding off here, as I'm sure any reader of Angel's purple prose has done many times before me, when I backtrack.

*Whoa.* Between the Half Moon Bay and the L.A. entries, she lived *where?* El Paso, Texas, for eight years? The Mr. Texas Muscle years? Same years—save one. Right out of junior college, she moved to El Paso.

"This ain't no coincidence," I say to the drywall, and it echoes back to me.

I'm sitting here congratulating myself for slogging through a letter I'll bet the police glazed over after the first ten words—if they looked at it at all—when all of a sudden I hear the click of three-inch heels on the basement stairs. It's Ardis, who doesn't impress me as a basement type, but I'm quite happy to see her instead of the Poundburns.

"Ruby. You said I could call you Ruby?"

"Of course." Well, she's not mad at me—that's something.

"I was on my way out to a luncheon appointment, but the girls at the desk told me you were waiting for someone from the management meeting. Hetty and Harmon had to leave, so they asked me to come down."

"No, I wasn't waiting for someone from the meeting—the receptionist was. She couldn't find Sonny Maples, so she let me come down and told me she'd let the managers know I was here."

"So you don't need me?"

As usual, she's in a hurry, which is fine with me. "No, I'm doing fine on my own. I have no idea why they felt Sonny had to be here."

Overkill. Why in the world did I blurt that out?

"Maybe Sonny wanted to tell you which files to look at—privacy, and all that."

"Well, apparently, the management let the police look at all these files when they were investigating Hubert Bogardis's part-time job here, so I don't know why he'd want to keep them out of the new computer system," I say.

More overkill. Why don't I just shut up and let her leave—I'm sure we'd both be happy.

"Well, I can't imagine they would have hired you if they hadn't wanted you to computerize the files. It's not my *area,* dear," she says on her way back up the stairs.

"Let's do lunch sometime," I yell up to her in Ardisspeak. I'd almost forgotten I'm supposed to get to know all these people better.

One thing's for sure—Ardis and Essie Sue are not as much alike as I thought. *Everything's* Essie Sue's *area*.

# 17

I've asked Kevin to pick me up tonight on his way to the Temple—I told him my car wasn't working. We're having a gathering of what I've come to call the Matzo Ball Committee—almost half the temple board. Most of them won't show up, of course, and that's fine with Essie Sue, who appointed them but doesn't expect them to get in the way of the detailed plans she's already made for the Ecumenical Diet Seder. Call me a rubber stamp, but now that I'm hot on the trail of Bogie's killer, I don't plan to miss a meeting.

Kevin's response to my call to hitch a ride was a rather bewildered "Huh?" I guess I don't ask him for lifts that often. Like never. He's responded more warily than I thought he would to my sudden attempt at being his new best friend. Oh, for the romance of yesteryear—call that last month—when he would have picked me up twenty minutes early just to enjoy more of my scintillating company. Tonight he whizzes by fifteen minutes late and roars off from the curb before I even have a chance to shut the door—not to mention buckling up. Could it be that my attraction is fading?

"You seem preoccupied, Kevin." I offer this after he fails to recognize my presence in the seat beside him until we're almost approaching the temple parking lot.

"Huh?"

Any thoughts I had of getting something out of him are rapidly dissipating.

"You've lost your touch, Ruby," I mutter out loud to myself. I didn't think you *could* mutter out loud, but I just did it. Boy, is he far gone. And I *have* lost my touch—I can't think of any way to bring up the ranch and the Angel thing. But since one of the main reasons I'm here is because I'm sure Angel will show up, I decide to wait until I see them together and hope something will come to me.

On the other hand, maybe Kevin's spaciness has nothing to do with Angel. If Paul's right, he knows more about Bogie's activities than he's saying, and holding back is making him nervous.

We hurry inside to the boardroom, where Essie Sue is tapping her longest two fingernails on the conference table while looking at her watch.

"You're the chairman, Rabbi," she whispers—if you can call that dull roar a whisper.

"Where's his cochairman?" I ask, remembering that's Angel.

"She's not here yet, either, but that's no excuse." She's looking at me as though it's my fault, and giving Kevin the perfect opening.

"I had to pick Ruby up."

The wimp.

"I knew it," Essie Sue says.

No, she didn't know it, and would never even suspect such a thing, but that's not stopping her from taking full advantage of it. She's just about to lay into me when Angel walks in.

"Sorry I'm late. I wasn't quite sure where I was going, and it's a long way from the ranch."

She doesn't seem to know where to sit down, and skips the seats beside me and Essie Sue. I can't say that I blame her—I think she's intimidated by both of us.

"Sit at the head of the table, by your cochairman," Essie Sue says.

Angel sits. I notice she and Kevin don't look at each other or exchange greetings. Then she says, "Hello, Rabbi," and he nods.

Not that this means a damn thing, and I know it, so I stop speculating.

Since both the chairman and cochair are now with us, it's Essie Sue who calls the meeting to order. Natch.

"Welcome to the Seder planning committee. We should begin with the food."

The Jewish way. Sounds reasonable. As if we'd have any say-so if it didn't.

"Look, people. Since this is a diet event, food becomes paramount."

We're expected to understand the logic of this, and believe it or not, we do.

"As you know, one of the symbols on the Seder plate is the egg, representing new life. But eggs contain too much cholesterol, so we're only planning on showing the egg. No one is to eat one."

Angel, the cochair, raises her hand for permission to speak. "That's wrong, Mrs. Margolis. Eggs have been proven to be safe if you only eat four a week. So we can ask people to save up."

"We'll table that." Essie Sue is not amused, but Angel doesn't get the full treatment, since Essie Sue needs someone from Fit and Rural on the committee.

"Next, people, we have to deal with that sweet wine. Passover wine is way too fattening and sweet, not to mention alcoholic. I suggest a substitute."

"No way." That's Mr. Chernoff, supported by six board members. Apparently, she's hit a collective nerve here.

"They said alcohol was bad last month on TV," Mrs. Chernoff reminds us. "It causes breast cancer. But yesterday in the paper they discovered a drink a day reduces the risk of heart disease. I move we should keep it."

Mr. Chernoff chimes in. "And we should keep the sweet Passover wine, too. I believe in tradition."

All the hands in the room go up. Fool with the food at your own risk, Essie Sue. Now they're emboldened, but that doesn't stop her from trying.

"It's *going* to be a diet Seder. We owe it to the community. And chicken is the low-fat alternative to red meat. We're having chicken."

Angel jumps up. "No. Chicken is contaminated with salmonella and campylobacter bacteria. Have you seen those assembly lines with the wrung necks?"

I'll bet Essie Sue's sorry she called this group together, but she keeps to her agenda. "And while we're on the subject, I just want to remind all of you how lucky we are to be having soup made with our wonderful diet matzo balls. If you remember nothing else from this meeting, people, don't forget that you should never, never nosh a matzo ball unless you know what's in it. Your health may be at stake."

"Salt is okay now. I heard it on PBS." That's Mrs. Levy.

"You can drop dead from it." Essie Sue pulls no punches. "And if this were a meal where we were serving butter, which we aren't, it would have to be replaced with margarine."

"No you don't." Angel's on her feet again. "Margarine's just as bad for your arteries, and worse even than butter."

"The food will be tabled, people. We're on to the Seder service in a minute, but a bigger priority is the folding chairs."

I have to give the woman credit. She knows when she's licked. Of course, since I'm sure she's planning to ignore all of them, she'll have the last calorie.

# 18

I don't like myself when I lurk, but there are times when I do it anyway. When the meeting's over, I tell Kevin I have to look up some lists in the temple office. Since I've outsmarted myself by asking him for a ride and thus depriving myself of my own car, this is the only way I can think of to give him a little time before he has to take me home. I want to see if Angel follows him to his study. She does, but so does Essie Sue. So far, I've seen absolutely nothing to make me think something's going on between Kevin and Angel. I'm beginning to think he wasn't the person in the car with her the other day.

My luck changes, though, when Essie Sue walks out of

his study with an armful of planning papers and leaves the door open.

"I'm off," she tells me at the door of the administrative office. "Hal has an appointment for his blood sugar tomorrow morning early, and I have to take him. If I don't, he won't remember half of what the doctor says."

Hal stopped remembering things years ago—I think she convinced him she could do a better job of it.

"Maybe we'll see you at the bakery—he has to fast until after the appointment, and then he likes his bagel as a reward. How do you think the meeting went?"

"Okay, I guess. I thought Kevin was supposed to chair it. Or Angel."

"They did chair it. They sat at the head of the table."

"No, you fielded all the questions and brought up all the issues. That's called chairing it."

"The rabbi's not good at that sort of thing—he lets people bully him."

I control myself and don't point my finger at the most obvious bully, who heads to the parking lot.

I decide to lurk at the children's water fountain, just around the corner from Kevin's study. I don't hear a thing—maybe they think everyone's gone. But that makes no sense, since he's got to take me home. Unless he's forgotten, which wouldn't surprise me in his present mood.

I don't know whether to saunter past the door or peek around the transom. I decide to saunter, since I have a legitimate excuse. If I expected a cozy scene, I was wrong. Kevin's sitting behind his behemoth of a desk, and Angel's sitting in the acolyte's chair beneath. Nothing's happening, but in its way, that's the oddest part of the scene. Both of them are quiet, just looking at each other when I pass the door. Kevin sees me first.

"Ruby—are you still here?"

Yep, I was right—he did forget.

"You probably forgot you brought me here," I say, causing Angel to turn around—either startled or annoyed—I can't tell which.

"Are you two planning to stay awhile? If so, I can always call a cab."

"No." They both speak at once.

"Well, then, if one of you can give me a lift whenever you're ready, I'll just wait in the library."

I'm not sure what my strategy is here—I'm making it up as I go. I guess I want to push a little, just to see if they even give a damn that they're not alone.

Angel gives first. "That's not at all necessary, Ruby. We were just talking over the meeting and deciding what needs to be done."

Kevin, whose every thought shows on his face, looks worried, then relieved at Angel's answer. Then he proceeds to spoil its effect.

"Yeah, yeah, she's right. That's what we were talking about. We were talking over the meeting and deciding what needs to be done."

Ditto would have been faster, but he doesn't think of that.

"So I guess you caught us cochairing," Angel says.

I caught 'em not talking is all, but the cover-up sure is getting interesting.

"So shall I just pull up a chair?"

They both jump up at once, so I guess a threesome is out.

"I'll take you home now." Kevin's halfway out the door.

"You're not just going to leave Angel here in the study, are you? Why don't the two of you come over for coffee?"

I certainly don't want Angel thinking I want to go out with Kevin for coffee. Or invite him home alone, either, for that matter. But she's having none of it.

"No, I have to go."

Kevin says nothing. Now that I think about it, the most interesting tidbit so far has been what they *haven't* said. He didn't even say good-bye to her when he rushed out the study door, which seems way more familiar than if he had.

He locks the building and we all go out to the parking lot, where Angel jumps in her car and I open Kevin's car door on the passenger side. I'm dying to see what he'll do next, because I'm sure they didn't expect to be separated this soon—and certainly not by me. He looks totally flummoxed, as if he doesn't know whether to climb in the driver's seat or stand outside.

He's rescued. "Oh, Rabbi—would you come over here for a minute?" Angel asks. "I forgot to ask you something."

The relief is visibly pouring out of him. Oh, yeah—I'm on to something.

He runs over to her car for about two seconds and runs back. I wave and we're on our way.

We don't talk on the way home, either—he's on another planet. But this time, it's fine with me. I can't wait until he drops me off. He screeches to a halt in front of my house after I remind him we've arrived.

"Well, see you later, Ruby."

"Thanks for the ride, Kevin. Would you mind staying here until I get in the house and turn on the lights? After all that trouble at my house after the temple fund-raising ball last year, I'm nervous."

I'm ready to repeat this in case he's still in space, but at least he responds this time.

"Sure, I'll wait."

"Until I turn the lights on."

"Yeah."

Yeah—if he waits until I get in the house and halfway into the garage before I turn on the lights, he won't have as big a head start on me.

When I follow him.

# 19

Kevin's car is easy to trail because he drives as though a big trough were on his right side and he were going to fall into it at any moment. Of course, this puts him hair-raisingly close to oncoming traffic, but apparently he doesn't mind drivers giving him the finger as his car rides the double yellow line. I try to stay two cars behind, which, at ten o'clock on a weeknight, means about two blocks in back of him. I'm not really worried about his seeing me—I've noticed he only uses the rearview mirror to check out his hair when he arrives at his destination.

My job is also easier because, unless they're meeting in a parking lot or driving to Austin, the number of places open after ten is, shall we say, limited. Like Denny's and the Sirloin Roundup—period. Since Austin is in the opposite direction of the guest ranch, I doubt they'll travel there this late. Of course, they could meet at his apartment. Or he could go to his place alone, if I'm totally wrong about this.

Kevin makes a crucial turn on Main Street, which, in Eternal, can only mean the Sirloin Roundup. His apartment's the other way. Call me unsentimental, but the idea of a tryst at the Sirloin Roundup is about as sexy as corned beef on white bread. Of course, *I'm* the one who's so sure it's a tryst. It's a measure of how much of a life I have that this entire little escapade could even intrigue me.

He swerves into the entrance driveway—as opposed to the exit driveway—a traffic pattern that presupposes actual traffic and represents a giant leap of faith on behalf of the management. I drive right on by and park next door at the brake shop. So far, I don't see Angel's car, but she's definitely there. If he wanted coffee by himself after the meeting, he'd go to Denny's—it's on the way to his apartment.

I snag my pants leg on the brick divider I have to climb over to get to the restaurant—this doesn't bode well, but it's too late now—I'm into this. Now I see Angel's car on the other side of the building. My on-the-fly P.I.ing hasn't included any advance planning, and I have no idea what I'm going to do next. Looking in the window seems as good as anything. Definitely *not* the long plate-glass window that runs the length of the building—they're probably at a table near it. But the entrance doors are the heavy, carved wooden kind, with glass panels on either side.

I run up to the entrance and fool with the empty newspaper machine as my excuse for standing there. Not that anyone would care—the place is totally empty. I look through one of the glass panels and see them sitting opposite each other in a booth. They're one of two couples in the whole place—about par for the course at one of our local nightspots. The only time I could have hoped to get into this place unseen would have been with the Sunday after-church crowd. Eavesdropping is out since I can't lip read—so now what?

No one is going to walk by here and disturb my perch beside the nonexistent newspapers, so I can take my time and just watch. Since there's no one in the place, their order comes pretty fast. Coffee, nachos for him, and fruit for her, it looks like. They're sharing. Whoa. They're *really* sharing—she's feeding him all the nachos.

Feeding him nachos *and* holding hands above the table—I hit the jackpot. Since there's nothing else I can do to prove my point that wouldn't be gross, the only thing left is to get out of here while I have plenty of time to get back to my car. This time, I sail over the divider, and I don't snag anything on the way to the car. I'm peculiarly giddy. Who'da thunk it? Kevin and Angel are an item.

Oy Vay's waiting for me when I get home, and we waste no time getting into the bedroom—she with her Milk-Bone, and me with my Diet Coke and the remains of the chopped liver Milt gave me this afternoon. I can't imagine why I don't have horrible nightmares when I eat this stuff, but I actually have more bad dreams on the nights I fall asleep on an empty stomach. Go know.

I gloat with Oy Vay over the fact that I've learned something Essie Sue doesn't know—a rare occurrence indeed. Wonder what she'll think. One thing's for certain—I'm off the hook for the dates from hell. Of course, almost as soon as I breathe easy over the discontinuation of our coupleness, another scene pops into my mind. I picture myself back in the basement of Fit and Rural, poring over those employment applications. Bogie in El Paso for nine years. Angel in El Paso for eight of those years. An awful big coincidence.

Another thought hits me at the same time—I'm feeling protective about Kevin, now that I won't have to dodge him anymore. He looked so happy when Angel was feeding him. Of course, I'm happy when I'm being fed, too, but still.

I want to know more about Angel's background. Maybe something's wrong with me, but I find it really hard to trust a woman whose conversation is constantly sprinkled with the word *Universe*.

# 20

I just saw my first celebrity at Fit and Rural—a familiar face that, natch, I couldn't place—I'm bad at faces, especially from movies and TV. She was all decked out in the logoed gym suit they give out here (except that they made me buy one to wear on the job)—beige and white with a navy emblem. I'm certain this is Ardis's doing—it matches the decor, and bears her stamp of "understated elegance." The Poundburns would no doubt prefer red and green, but it looks as though they lost out on this one. The entire layout of the spa is schizophrenic in this respect—wild bursts of French Provincial alternating with white on white.

I ask the receptionist who the woman is.

"Oh, that's Charmain Gill—she played that other daughter on *Dallas*. Doesn't she look great for her age?"

I guess that depends on how old she really is under the face-lifts. She's certainly thin for her age—for any age.

"Why's she here?" I ask. Certainly not to stay a size three—size three would engulf this woman.

"Probably just for R&R. Lots of them like to soak in the ambience of the place."

To each her own. I'm just glad to see some sign of life around here. I'm on my way to a conference with my boss, Sonny, about the database—a chaperoned meeting, I hope. On the way down the hall I glimpse the glassed-in aerobics room, where to my surprise, at least twenty beige-and-white-clad exercisers are going at it on the stair steps. Things *are* picking up.

I peek into Sonny's office, but he's late, as usual—if he shows up at all. I decide to walk around his desk while I wait. He's not very messy—no revealing telephone messages stuck on skewers like in the old movies. It occurs to me that no one leaves phone messages anymore—it's the answering machine or e-mail—not exactly a casual snooper's paradise. The window behind Sonny's desk looks out on the back patio, though, and I can see some workers setting dishes out on a long folding table. They must be previewing the upcoming Seder.

It's almost lunchtime, and I don't sense any signs of life down the corridor—either they've all left for lunch dates or they're actually trying out the new chef's fare, such as it is. I haven't had the pleasure yet, but the word is her cuisine gives new meaning to the word *nouvelle*. I hear a magnifying glass is part of the place setting.

I realize this might be a great time to explore some of the rooms that weren't part of the guided tour. I found a real bonanza in the file room the other day when I discovered a complete set of plans for the ranch. I photocopied one of the simpler one-page drawings, and looked over the rest to get a feel for the place. The kitchen wing is more extensive than the part Harmon showed me. I'm a bit hesitant to explore during lunchtime, but maybe the busiest time would be the best—lots of movement going on and nobody paying attention.

For the first time, I'm glad to be wearing this Fit and Rural outfit—they made me buy the pants and jacket, too, but today I just have on the shorts and polo shirt, so I look even more like a guest. I cross from the administrative wing to the kitchen wing by the outside path—the best way to avoid the dining room, I'm hoping. I have my choice of several back doors. One leads directly to the kitchen, where I can see through the window that the new chef is busy wielding whatever it is she wields, with lots of activity around her.

I choose a door to the storage area. Yep, this is the perfect time. I slip in totally unnoticed, and find myself in the same cool, new, and sawdusty atmosphere as the basement filing room. Boxes are piled to the ceiling—the ones I can see contain cleaning supplies and paper goods. I feel a bit foolish not knowing what I'm after. Nan's original observation in e-mail was that a guest ranch with so few clients needed looking into, but now the place looks alive and well.

I walk down the corridor. No one's around anyway, and if someone sees me, I can always say I'm on my way to lunch. The cold room is on my right, and I try the door just to see—it's open. There's a big, burly guy in there who looks like a butcher—he's wearing a white bib apron, white pants, and a white tee shirt. He's going in and out of the adjoining walk-in freezer, checking the frozen food, including the whole wall of Essie Sue's diet matzo balls I saw last time, and he's writing on a yellow pad. The Poundburns showed me those cartons the other day, so I figure that's as good an excuse as any to go in.

When I walk into the cold room, he jumps.

"Sorry—I didn't mean to startle you. The Poundburns showed me these rooms. You seem to have even more of our cartons than last time I looked."

"What are you doing in here?"

"I work here. And I'm also helping with the matzo ball sales. Who are you?"

"Never mind who I am. I want you out of here."

Two beefy arms shove me out the door—not that I'm too sorry—it's colder in there than I remembered. He comes out with me, and locks the door behind him. Now I see his name—Bud—on a tag pinned to his shirt.

"So what's the big secret, Bud?" I say. "As I told you, the Poundburns—"

"You had no business going near that freezer." This guy's scary.

"What do you have in there—bodies? The door was open to the cold room, and you were in there. I wasn't sneaking in." Not that I wouldn't have, but he doesn't have to know that. What *is* the big deal?

He looks as if he's ready to freeze *me* for storage, so I decide to move on.

I do a quick "Sorry I disturbed you, Bud," and cut across the corridor to what turns out to be a door off the dining room before he can ask me my name.

The dining room's buzzing. At least half the tables are filled, and some of the people whose names I've just been taking in vain are sitting around one of the tables in the middle of the room. I can see Hetty and Harmon at the head and foot of the table holding court—and more important, they can see me. So I relax and play it out—not that I have a choice. Besides the Poundburns and some guests I don't know, Ardis and the elusive Sonny are there. I guess this is my chance to try the cuisine.

"Can I join you?" There are seats to spare, so after nodding to everyone, I grab the chair next to Sonny and start talking.

"We had an appointment this morning, but you weren't in your office."

Sonny can be counted on never to apologize. "Yeah, I had to be somewhere."

"So can we have a quick meeting now?" I'm avoiding any introductory remarks from Harmon, such as where was I coming from, and it seems to be working.

"It can wait. We've just ordered."

Not to be left out—especially when there's food around—I wave the waitress over and ask to look at a menu. I have three choices, and they're certainly surprising ones:

*Old-Fashioned Barbecued Hot Dog*
*Juicy Fit and Rural Burger*
*Tuna Melt Surprise*

"Where's the fruit and cottage cheese?" I ask.

"Too boring," the waitress shoots back at me. "We want to teach you to enjoy ordinary good American food."

"Hey, you won't get an argument out of me." Maybe I prejudged the chef. "I'll take the hot dog."

Ardis is nodding her approval, which really confuses me.

"This doesn't sound like your style, Ardis."

"I ordered the tuna surprise," she says, "but yours is good, too."

I notice there are no prices on the menu—just a calorie count, including fat and fiber grams. What a deal.

The waitress comes back to the table with a tray full of what looks like seven shot glasses full of tomato juice.

"The Bloody Marys," she announces. We all drink up. I don't have enough of mine to taste, but I'd say it's about ninety percent Tabasco sauce.

"That was it?"

They all look at me. "The first course," Harmon says.

When in Rome, I guess. I decide to keep my mouth shut, and I'm even desperate enough to wish Kevin were here for support. He likes real food—wasn't Angel just feeding him nachos not long ago? Now that I think of it, why *was* she feeding him nachos?

Sonny's paying no attention to me, and neither is anyone else, for that matter. This dining experience is about as much fun as the third wedding dinner on a busy weekend. And the food's not as good. I withhold judgment, though, because the main course is headed our way, heralded by a detailed description of each dish by the waitress.

My old-fashioned barbecued hot dog turns out to be a three-inch-long soybean log cleverly nestled in its bun: a split yellow summer squash. The whole thing is covered with a suspicious-looking brown "barbecue" sauce made from unsweetened cocoa mixed with a soupçon of Diet Pepsi. A toothpick holds it all together. The bad news is that the brown sauce makes it impossible to get to the squash, which may have been edible. The good news is that the toothpick is normal—and not bad, either.

I can't fake this, even to keep my job, but everyone else seems to be tearing into the food with gusto. I try to make up for not eating by doing most of the talking, and, as usual, Ardis seems the most likely to respond without snarling.

"Do they repeat these menus during the session, or come up with new ones every day?" I ask her.

Hetty interrupts. "We make up every one of these," she says. "I personally work with the chef."

That explains it. Just as I'm thinking of a response, Bud, the look-alike butcher, crosses the room and heads to our table. He whispers in Harmon's ear, keeping his eyes on me. Harmon shoots straight up out of his chair and follows him from the room, with Hetty right behind.

I'm hoping Sonny and Ardis didn't notice the looks

directed my way, and I make my excuses—telling Sonny we'll meet whenever he wants, which I've already noticed doesn't seem to be now. What I'm wondering is why it took Bud so long to get in here. My inclination is to take off for home, but I might be able to learn a lot more by staying.

I go down to the file room in the administration wing and scoop up a bunch of forms for the database, so I'll have something that looks like work in my hands. Then I cross back over by the same outside route to the back door of the kitchen storage room and cold room. Thanks to the cheap construction of these new buildings, I might be able to hear Harmon and Bud.

Nope, not a sound. If they're in the freezer, I can forget the eavesdropping, but why would they want to subject themselves to the cold for any longer than necessary? On the outside chance they're somewhere audible, I crack open the door from the storage room to the hallway. Bingo.

"Of course, I brought her by here." Harmon's Texas drawl sounds less Texan, but it could be because he's not giving a canned spiel. "She was supposed to be checking on the work for Mrs. Margolis. What business is it of yours how I handle this?"

"I don't think she should have been brought here at all. You could have shown her a sample carton in your office."

"Give it a rest, Bud. Just do your work."

"With her following me in here?"

"Whose fault was that? You left the door unlocked behind you."

"I don't like it. Hey—what was that noise?"

Nothing from my direction, but I'm taking no chances. As I close the door, I hear Harmon saying, "It's only Hetty. Can't she trust me to do anything on my own?"

I do know I have to get back in that cold room, but it's gonna take some planning, and since the Seder date is just around the corner, I might have to wait. Right now, I'm outta here. I close the door and scoot out the other exit to the outside, carrying home a lot of extra papers I don't need—but that's the least of my worries.

# 21

I walk into Temple a little late. Friday night services at Temple with Kevin in the pulpit usually draw about fifty people, but tonight we have at least a hundred and fifty. Since there's no major event planned, I'm wondering what the buzz is. Whatever it is, I'm definitely out of the loop—I haven't heard a shred of casual conversation about anything special going on.

I'm looking around me with amazement—not only is the temple board here, but all the members of the fundraising committee have shown up. In the back of the room is a whole contingent from Fit and Rural, most of whom aren't even Jewish. Word of mouth, whatever it is, can really bring 'em out in Eternal.

Tonight's message was billed in the temple bulletin as "The Twenty-first Century and Me," not an unusual title to the regular bulletin readers, since our rabbi's most enthusiastic sermons are about himself. But I can't imagine the topic has generated such an outpouring. Essie Sue Margolis is the only officer sitting in the pulpit with Kevin. She's wearing a chic beige sweater dress and looks ready for action. I'm getting uneasy. Whatever the new project is, I hope it doesn't mean more work. Millennially speaking, I haven't quite recovered from the twentieth century, much less this new one.

I can tell Kevin's excited, because he races through the liturgy with a pace approaching the speed of light. I usually enjoy the meditative quality of the ritual, but not when I'm herded up and down for the prayers so fast I'm out of breath. Essie Sue's the only one in the congregation who's keeping up with him. In fact, I can see her giving him hand signals to move faster.

By the time there's a pause before announcements and the sermon, we're all exhausted. Essie Sue goes to the pulpit.

"Ladies and gentlemen, I want to welcome such an overwhelming crowd here tonight—it just goes to show that Judaism is alive and well in Eternal."

I'm thinking it might show that one particular Jew has been making a lot of phone calls, and I'm dying to know why. She confirms my observation.

"Our event tonight came too late to be put in the bulletin, so I spread the news the old-fashioned way—I telephoned as many people as I could reach, and asked them to tell others. I know you're all anxious to know what we're celebrating, so I won't keep you in suspense.

"It is my distinct pleasure to announce that our own Rabbi Kapstein has become engaged to Miss Angel Elkin, newly of this city. Miss Elkin serves as spiritual director of the Fit and Rural Reducing Ranch, Central Texas's leading residential reducing facility. Her profession is most fitting for her future role as wife to our rabbi. Will you join us, Angel?"

Well, you can knock me over with a wet falafel. Some snoop I am—here I thought I was the only one who knew about the romance, and Essie Sue's talking engagement already.

Kevin is beaming as Angel ascends the stairs to the pulpit. She's looking very spiritual in an ankle-length flowered dress with matching flowered halo circling her head. Her hair is waved down to mid-back and entangled with artificial bluebonnets. Her toenails are painted pink and are encased in blue suede Birkenstocks.

The more I think about this, the more startling it is that they've enlisted Essie Sue already—I never thought of Angel as her type. Of course, that she's Kevin's type is more important, but I'm still surprised they managed to get Essie Sue's approval so quickly. There must be a story behind this.

Essie Sue leads Angel to her chair and Kevin steps up to the lectern. He's obviously thrilled, and I'm happy for him. At the same time, it's a little soon, in my opinion, for the big step, and I'm hoping it's a long engagement. After all, what does he know about her?

Kevin greets the congregation, then launches into his sermon. We hear all about the New Century and Kevin, and the exciting life he'll embark upon with Angel. I guess it *is* appropriate, in that sense.

"Yes, ladies and gentlemen, that's right. We can all grow and learn from our loved ones. Since my fiancée, Angel Elkin, is a spiritual leader in her own right, she has taught me a great deal already. I have absorbed her compassion and universality. Angel has convinced me that certain concepts are far too harsh for the first years of the emerging century. I'll let her tell you herself."

Angel flows to the lectern. Since I've been treated several times to her brand of spirituality, I'm not paying the closest attention. I'm mellowing out and letting it wash over me, when I do a double take. She said *what?*

"Yes, my fellow seekers, it's time for a change. The Ten Commandments has had its day. At the dawn of a gentler century, wiser souls are persuading the world with the Ten Suggestions. How much more readily they would be accepted than the authoritarian concepts of yesteryear."

She's off and running—or running off—take your pick. I notice that most of the congregation haven't been paying too much attention, either, but a few people are beginning to whisper over this one. Even Essie Sue has perked up—yikes, she's looking at me. Yeah—*now* she wants my advice.

Angel's just warming up.

"Take *Thou shalt not kill*—you know? I mean, look at

O.J.—'If the glove fits, thou shalt convict'—or something like that. But it didn't fit, and they couldn't convict. And that policeman was so *prejudiced*. I mean, it's all relative, right?"

Essie Sue's looking to the rabbi for help now, but he's mesmerized.

"And *Thou shalt not commit adultery*—do you see where I'm going here? This is the laid-back generation—maybe what you call adultery, another person, with as much right as you to have an opinion, would just call it fooling around, or really, really special affection, you know? And how about people who are just born to hug?"

The place is finally awake. I'm glad there are no tomatoes on the Oneg Shabbat table.

"And after Menendez, I mean, who could honor *that* father and mother?"

Essie Sue's getting no help from the pulpit, so she acts alone.

"Thank you, Angel. The rabbi will now continue with the service."

"But I haven't discussed *Just say no* yet. How about *Just say maybe?* It's more humane."

Angel won't back down. But Essie Sue, who knows from the First Commandment but not the First Amendment, is stronger than she is. She drags Angel back to her chair and motions to Kevin, who gets to the mike faster than a speeding bullet.

"Uh, how about a song before we finish the service?"

In my opinion, we need a hook.

I think Angel, Essie Sue, and the rabbi were all supposed to shake hands in the receiving line, but Essie Sue finesses this by asking Angel to come help cut the cake. Wise move.

As I pass her at the tea table, I give Essie Sue her due. "You certainly kept a fine secret tonight," I say.

"Ruby, I told you if you didn't think the rabbi was a good catch, someone else would," she snaps.

Oh, I get it. I'm being punished.

"Then you must be very happy now," I say sweetly.

From the looks of her, I think this match point is mine.

# 22

E-mail from: Ruby
To: Nan
Subject: *Weddings and Weirdos*

In answer to your last question, so far I haven't heard any wedding plans—I promised to keep you posted, and I will, although it's probably a little early. Kevin's ecstatic that Essie Sue jumped right into the engagement plans, although that *was* before last week's temple fiasco. I'll bet now she's rethinking her strategy of being an early mentor to the happy couple and thus able to have a hand in all the goodies to come.

I get reports that she's still recovering from the Ten Suggestions, and I'll bet she's wondering how she's going to keep her hands on the reins when Angel the Space Cadet is in the driver's seat. How's *that* for mixed metaphors? At any rate, this might be one plan that backfires on her.

E-mail from: Nan
To: Ruby
Subject: *Torts and Other Terrors*

I need a break from school. There are days I can't believe I got myself into this. And as for thinking I had a leg up because I worked in a law office—forget it. The word is that my experience will be helpful *after* law school—now they tell me.

Yeah—Essie Sue must be kicking herself for helping bring Angel on board. Does she have you running back and forth getting ready for that fat-farm Seder on the first night of Passover? Maybe you can get Paul Lundy invited and the two of you can nose around between courses.

E-mail from: Ruby
To: Nan
Subject: *Seder Number Three*

I need to discover what's such a big

secret at my new place of employment. Paul Lundy wouldn't be caught dead at one of Essie Sue's extravaganzas, but now and then, he reminds me that I volunteered to be his eyes and ears there. He's following up on information from Bogie's and Angel's personnel files, but what he wants from me is some one-to-one networking. Let's call that networking what it is—good old reliable office gossip. It seems odd to Paul that the Poundburns are still secretive about Bogie's employment even though he's dead and his moonlighting is no longer an issue.

The Ecumenical Diet Seder is the third night of Passover, believe it or not. The first night we have the home Seder, then there's the regular Seder for temple members on the second night, and Essie Sue's reserved the third night for this Ecumenical Diet Seder. This is not to mention Mock Seders for the kids, Demo Seders for novices, and Seders given by church groups. Passover's so *in* these days I'm surprised we have enough nights to go around.

I *do* plan to nose around, though—as you so delicately put it. I'm hoping so much will be going on, no one will notice.

# 23

It's a good thing I've already attended two Seders this week—otherwise, I'd have a hard time relating tonight's event to anything remotely resembling Passover. For openers, the idea of an outdoor Seder doesn't exactly grab me. Essie Sue, eschewing paper goods for the outdoors, has decreed plastic as the tableware of choice—she says it's dressier. The committee could find only one plastic item embossed with a Passover emblem—the translucent purple drinking cups are stamped with bunches of grapes. News flash—these weren't Passover cups, but Ann Helfman, the titular chairperson, swore they were, and we all backed her up. I say *titular* because we all know who the real chairperson is, and unless that's understood, nothing gets done.

We almost had a resignation over the head table. Ann decided to put some of the honorary guests at each table, but our rabbi wanted all the ministers at the head. Besides causing major clerical overload, this arrangement would have meant no room for the members who had been chosen to help lead the service. Happily for me, I realize I don't have to be concerned about this anymore.

Kevin's halfway through the first portion of the Seder service—I don't know why he's racing, except that maybe he's hungry and wants to get to the dinner part. He's lost several pounds on his diet. Since we're serving skinless chicken, unadorned veggies, and a defatted matzo meal pudding, which is now so congealed it could hold a building together, I'm sure he won't gain any weight tonight. I could tell the food had passed muster by the Fit and Rural head chef when I cruised by the kitchen tonight and didn't smell anything cooking. None of those wonderful crispy odors associated with the holiday have survived the caloric apocalypse. You can't broil Styrofoam.

One of the children present has just raised her hand to ask how we're going to be able to open the door later for the prophet Elijah, since we're in the woods. Not exactly in the woods, but since this gigantic patio is the only part of the landscape that's been graded, I'd say we're pretty close.

Angel jumps up.

"Opening the door for Elijah is such an integral part of the Seder that I'm sure this won't be a problem. We're all supposed to imagine he's been let in and out, so now we can just imagine that we're imagining it."

Makes sense to me. Kevin's nodding *yes,* so I guess it's a done deal. Essie Sue's oblivious to the niceties of the service—she's only interested in plugging the diet matzo balls.

"After you people have tasted the wonderful soup we're passing, I know you'll want to pick up an extra carton of our reduced-fat matzo balls. Members of the Fit and Rural staff will be on hand to fill your orders. Remember our slogan—a matzo ball a day keeps a heart attack away."

Neither original nor accurate, but that's never stopped her before. I doubt most of our Seder participants are going to be panting for more matzo balls. Having sat through two Seders already this week, the Jews in the crowd are glassy-eyed, and the visitors are frankly still chewing. Trust me, there's nothing chewier than dry meal that's been frozen and then boiled. Eggs give it moisture, but of course they've been banned. Essie Sue's had her way with the wine, too—she's even found grape juice with aspartame.

Since dinner's about to be served, maybe this would be a good time to do my exploring. The kitchen's obviously busy, and I'll bet the cold room is hopping, too. Bud couldn't possibly be keeping people out of there tonight.

The Poundburns are helping oversee the waiters and waitresses—I can see them both by the serving table. Tonight they're once again in full western regalia, minus the cowboy hats. I guess that's supposed to be some sign of respect for the occasion. Sonny and Ardis are seated at one of the side tables—she's a bit formal in a good-looking navy dress, but who *would* know what to wear for an event like this? I feel sorry for all the men who figured a suit would be appropriate for a Seder ceremony—they're apparently sweltering, and I see a lot of ties under tables.

Angel and Kevin are feeding each other matzo ball soup—nice that someone's happy with it. This looks like the perfect opportunity for me to take off.

I've picked exactly the right time to explore the kitchen area—workers are busy dishing out serving platters and paying absolutely no attention to me. The Fit and Rural service staff is outnumbered by the temple and church volunteers, making for one humongous mess, if you ask me. It's easy to slip next door into the cold room, where the door's been wedged open by a block of wood.

Although I'm thrilled that some of the warm air is making the room more comfortable, I shudder to think what it's doing to the bacteria count. The whole matzo ball project could come to a screeching halt if people begin dropping like flies. I'm making a mental note to close the door when I leave, but for now, I doubt that two more minutes will make a difference.

The lights are on in here, and I'm not worried about getting caught. In the general melee, I can always say I was sent to bring out more cartons to the kitchen. I *am* afraid of Bud finding me again, but he seemed to be very busy on the patio when I left. I'm headed toward the freezer room where the cartons were piled the first time I ever saw this place.

Most of the cartons are unmarked—I guess those are

for local distribution. Essie Sue told me that the Fit and Rural staff is freezing and packaging the matzo balls and delivering them back to her kitchen at the Center. From there, the local customers can pick them up and the delivery service can express the out-of-town orders. Essie Sue's Center is a more convenient pickup point for the Eternal customers than Fit and Rural would be.

I can't even imagine whom Essie Sue might have commandeered to order the matzo balls from out of town—I personally wouldn't be caught dead receiving frozen goods that way—but mine's not to question why. Fit and Rural is handling the orders, and apparently, Essie Sue's already received some good-sized weekly checks, so what do I know?

I see several boxes ready for shipping—labels and all. They're loaded two cartons deep on a few of the bottom shelves. Nosy Parker that I am, I shove a couple of them around to see where they're going. All the places she has relatives, I'm sure. I take out the pen and paper I've brought along in my pocket and start listing the destinations, when I hear voices. I know someone will come to find me if I stay here too long—I'd better get out of here. Not to mention that even a few minutes in here is almost intolerable.

As I leave, I shut the door tight to keep the room cold—hopefully protecting a few of the unfortunate recipients of these frozen goodies. If this were one of my favorite murder mysteries, I'd no doubt be shivering on the other side of this door, locked in with the missing bodies. In fact, if I have to listen to more of Angel's ecumenical explanations of Passover lore, I might *prefer* being blocked in ice. Maybe I've missed most of the festivities—I know I've definitely avoided the diet dinner, which is a bonus in itself.

Nothing looks out of place here, so I slip back to my table wearing my I've-never-been-gone look, but it doesn't fool Essie Sue.

"So where have you been?" She's cornered me—if she moves any closer, my flimsy metal chair is going to fold over backward.

"I was helping with the serving." She's not buying any.

"I didn't see you going in and out of the kitchen at all. You've missed most of the Seder, and I was going to call on you to read. Pastor Hearn was struggling with the Hebrew."

"You gave the guests the Hebrew portions?" I struggle, but I'm in no mood to fight. Not after my third Seder this week.

She ignores me, as usual, so I change the subject. "Were you pleased with the way the Seder went, Essie Sue?"

"Onward and upward."

I guess I'm supposed to decipher that, but I take it as an exit line, and go look for Kevin.

He and Angel are holding hands and accepting congratulations from the guests. They must have announced the engagement again, which means they haven't changed their minds. I wait to approach Kevin until Angel's deep in conversation with one of the visitors. He's definitely lost some weight—in fact, his face looks a bit gaunt, but he seems fit enough.

"Where were you, Ruby? Essie Sue was looking for

you." Kevin looks undaunted after conducting three Seders in a row.

"I was in the kitchen. Do you know much about the matzo ball cartons stored in the freezer here?"

"Just that they truck them back to Essie Sue's Center to be picked up. Why?"

I started this conversation, and now I don't know quite where to go with it. I was hoping maybe he knew more than I did because of his connection with Angel. But since she was so tight-lipped when she visited my house a while back, I don't want to say anything to her.

"Ruby," Kevin says, changing the subject back to himself, "I know you're upset over the turn of events that's culminated in my engagement. I just want you to know that Angel understands fully why you and I broke up."

*Oy*. Broke up? The hairs on the back of my neck are already rising when I realize nothing I say is going to change his mind. The more I protest that we weren't a couple, the more I'll be reminded of our first dance and other horrors. Besides, if he and Angel feel sorry for me, maybe I can put that to use in having her open up to me.

"Well, I understand fully, too, Kevin," I confess as Angel approaches us. At least, I thought she was headed toward us. She's not. She sails right to Kevin, takes his arm, and drags him away. So much for her full understanding.

I'm a woman scorned.

# 24

At last—a teeny, tiny job perk at the fat farm. Not that I necessarily deserve any perks—I haven't been working here long, and I'm using the job to possibly learn more about Bogie's murder, but as they say, never turn down geeks bearing gifts.

Today I've been offered a practice massage from Svetlana, a recent Russian immigrant, who, despite no doubt being mightily underpaid by Hetty and Harmon, is wildly enthusiastic about pounding flesh. I gather she's definitely not from the subtle school of massage arts, but I'm up for it—frankly, I need the kneading.

The event is taking place in the late afternoon, within a

semi-private cubicle that's part of the gymnasium wing of Fit and Rural. I say *semi-private* because a strung-up blue sheet is dividing the already small room, and I can hear the sound of a table being moved around on the other side for yet another customer—maybe even a free one like me. I'm lying facedown on a slab that has an attachment at one end resembling a wooden toilet seat. My forehead and chin rest on the wooden frame, leaving my nose and mouth free to presumably take in air.

Either Svetlana's the strong, silent type or she speaks no English—at any rate, we've gotten this far by sign language. She slathers pungent oil on me—I've never smelled liniment, but I'm sure this is it. The stuff burns, but I'm cool about it. I don't believe in looking a gift horse in the mouth (not that I could from this position) even if I strongly suspect the creature's liniment is being used on me. They don't call this place a ranch for nothing.

Svetlana's tough. As she proceeds to probe my spinal cord in ways that would make even a KGB agent surrender, I notice that she does know two English phrases—*you relex,* and *big knots*. I interpret her frequent repetitions to mean that my body contains many, many *big knots,* and that I need to *relex*. Trust me, Svetlana—if you weren't finding so many big knots, I would be able to relex.

I've fallen asleep on many a massage table, but there's no way this is going to happen here. For one thing, I want to be conscious if nerve damage strikes—but I couldn't fall asleep if I wanted to, because another Russian has taken charge on the other side of the sheet—a very loud Russian.

"Who?" I point.

"Husband." After which she proceeds to begin a long, loud conversation with her spouse in Russian, punctuated on both sides of the sheet with many slaps on prone flesh.

I listen hard for any signs of the English language on Husband's part, and finally conclude, to my shock and surprise, that his two phrases are *roll over* and *rabbi*. *Oy*—Kevin is my massage-mate.

I decide that I really have no desire to converse with Kevin over the Russian roar—I'll leave well enough alone and concentrate on the much more important task of avoiding paralysis at the hands of Svetlana. I'll leave Kevin to deal with his own neurological problems.

It's time for me also to roll over, though there's no word for it on this side—just a shove that almost takes my nose off, since I forget to lift my face out of its wooden frame. Now that Svetlana has me sunny-side up, she's oiling my toes, which are very ticklish, and they react in Pavlovian fashion, totally out of my control. In other words, I kick her. A barrage of Russian ensues, and Husband invades my private space to protect Wife. I roll over again faster than an oiled bullet, wrapping myself in the sheet that was loosely covering me, and emitting my own barrage in English—which, of course, shatters my anonymity across the sheet.

"Ruby? Is that you? You're interrupting my massage. Angel says a massage is supposed to be quiet and meditative."

I have to sit up over this one. "Kevin, if you can tell me this has been a quiet, meditative experience up to now, you're acoustically challenged."

I use my feet to push Husband back through the sheet, where he immediately issues a commanding "Rabbi, roll over." Svetlana urges me to relex, and all is quiet on both sides.

Kevin and I are both presumably drifting off peacefully when Husband barks, "Facial," in a voice that could raise a corpse.

I'm being turned over once more, and a soothing brown goo is sculpted over my face. It looks and smells like café au lait with cinnamon. I'm assuming Kevin is getting the same treatment. As the glop begins to harden, I try to speak, but realize I can't. Svetlana places a wet cloth over my nose and mouth. The last thing I know is that another odor is mixing with the cinnamon. It's ether.

# 25

I awake with the mother of all headaches. A chorus line of frozen matzo balls is dancing past my left eye, over the bridge of my nose, and beyond my right eye to infinity—or to my right ear—whichever comes first. When I close my eyes to try to get away from the matzo balls, they turn into floaters just behind my eyelids. Very cold floaters.

I try to go back to sleep so I can avoid something. At first I think I'm avoiding the pain, but then the cold becomes worse than the pain. Finally, they're both doing a job on me. I curl up like a ball, but the ball hurts. I stretch out my arms and legs, but the hands and feet on the ends of them turn to ice.

When Joshie was eleven, he wrote a country western song—"It Hurts When You're Cold to Me." I try to sing it behind the cowboy kerchief over my nose.

*Baby, baby, baby,*
*Can't you see,*
*It hurts, hurts, hurts,*
*When you're cold to me.*

I can't hear myself, and my lips won't move when I sing. Now I feel like a slab of meat in a butcher shop. I don't know what to do, so I just lie here and try to sleep. I wonder where *here* is.

My eyes are opening, and I attempt to sit up. I'm looking at matzo balls. Not this again. I must have been asleep, but now I feel wide awake, and the matzo balls aren't dancing. I can see them in an adjoining room, through some sort of glass or heavy Plexiglas wall, neatly packed in their cartons on shelves. I start to raise myself, and the matzo balls do dance for a minute or so, but then they settle down when I decide to stay put. I'm sitting on the floor, dressed in a royal blue sweat suit with the *F&R* logo on it. I have on a pair of white cotton crew socks. None of these clothes are mine, and they're way too big.

Even though I'm awake, my mind and body aren't quite under my control. One minute I'm sitting cross-legged, calmly looking around me, and the next minute I'm reaching for a blanket. Or a quilt, or the feather comforter on top of my bed at home. Or for Oy Vay, who's very large and warm and huggable.

I get dizzy when I turn too fast, so I stay where I am. Then curiosity gets the better of me, and I slide myself around in a semicircle. The floor is nice and smooth, and my sweatpants can swivel with ease.

Across the room, I see a rolled-up pink blanket, but my sense of it is fuzzy, and the room seems to be getting darker by the minute. The blanket becomes a pink blob, and bobs and weaves before me. I don't think I can stand up to go get it, so I use that sliding motion to propel myself. The movement makes me dizzy, but I want the blanket. For the first time, I realize with full consciousness how cold I am.

I know something's not right with my insides when I discover that even in the midst of this big chill, I'm sweating from the mere effort of moving across the room. When I'm finally able to reach out for the pink blanket, my hand touches something bristly instead of the softness I'm expecting. Whoa. It's bristly *and* it just rolled over.

"Ruby—what have you done to me?"

I'm freezing, my eyes are seeing double, and I'm being blamed for something. It must be Kevin.

I think the bristles I touched were his five o'clock shadow—or who knows what o'clock—I blink my eyes to clear up the fog and see if I can tell from the growth of his beard how long we've been in here. The growth isn't all that thick, but the rest of him is quite a sight in a bright pink sweat suit about three sizes too small. Since my own outfit is huge on me and undoubtedly blue for boy, I can only surmise that there was a mix-up and whoever dressed us in these getups was in a big hurry.

"I didn't do anything to you, Kevin—obviously, we've both been had in some way I'm too fuzzy to figure out yet. Uh—would you like to sit a little closer, or am I the only one who's turning into an ice cube?" Getting some warmth from his body while we wait is worth having to hear him remind me he's an engaged man.

Hey—wait for *what?* I'm extremely slow on the uptake here, but it's dawning on me that I need to get moving, in more ways than one.

Kevin's not too swift, either, and just gives me a blank stare. But he does let me lean against him. I get one quick shot of body warmth, and then use his bulk to push off from as I try to stand up. It's dark in here, but seeable—although it seems to be getting darker than it was earlier when I saw the rows of matzo balls. There's a dim light coming from somewhere off to the side of the room. I head toward it in slow motion—it's a window high up, with decorative metal curlicues covering it. At this point, I'm more interested in finding a door.

"Get up, Kevin. Help me look for a way out of here."

"How did we get in here?"

"I don't think we should worry about that now. We need to get out. *Out,* Kevin—look for *out.*" I think he's in shock—not that I'm not, but I'm hoping he'll respond to simple commands. He does, and makes a faint effort to get up. I pull at him and almost lose my own balance, but he makes it.

I take his arm and decide I'll be better off if I use him as a walking aid. Besides, it's scary in here, and I'm glad I'm not alone—although I have to admit this is about as alone as you can get in the presence of another person. Unfortunately, I'm in no position to be choosy.

I take a route that follows the wall, and all along the way I look and feel for a light switch before the room dims even more. The light's fading so fast it must be dusk. No light switch, but we do seem to be approaching a glassed-in portion of the room. My mind has finally cleared enough to know for sure that we're in the refrigerated room that's visible from the kitchen, assuming anyone's around to look.

I remember now that we have to be approaching the door—it was near the glass wall.

"A few more steps, Kevin. I know where the door is."

He's not saying anything.

"Kevin? Look at me. Are you hurting?"

He looks at me like I'm nuts. "Hurting? Just all over."

"Yeah, I know, but I don't mean that. Do you have any specific hurts, like an awful headache?"

I'm figuring he may have a concussion.

"No. No headache."

I guess he doesn't have a head injury. My head doesn't hurt as much anymore, either, so I suppose we weren't hit over the head and dragged in here. I decide to quit diagnosing when I realize that this man wouldn't be any great shakes in the help department with or without a concussion. Lucky Angel.

I'd feel better if I could recollect how we got in here in the first place, but I have no memory of what I was doing today. Or yesterday, or whatever the time frame is. Not that it matters much.

"Here it is, Kevin." I reach for the doorknob and it moves freely. Too freely. The knob turns but the door's not budging.

"You want to see if you can throw yourself at it?" I ask him. Wishful thinking, but I'm desperate. He gives a half-hearted shove with his shoulder and, of course, accomplishes nothing. Where's Elijah when we need him? No doubt on leave from slipping through every Jewish doorway in the world on Passover.

So we're locked in. I'm thinking of all those questionnaires asking who you'd most like being trapped on a desert island with. I look over at my fellow prisoner. With one hand he's scratching himself as if I weren't standing here. With the other hand, he's either biting his thumbnail or doing a pretty good job of sucking his thumb. This Is Your Life, Ruby Rothman. The Karma from Hell. Except that I think karma's supposed to take the place of hell. I'll ask Angel, if I ever get out of here.

Enough wishful thinking—I forgo any help from Kevin, and head for some wooden packing cases on the far side of the room. I empty all the cartons from one of the cases, take it over to the glass wall, and fling it. All my smashing doesn't make a dent—this stuff must be bulletproof. My burst of energy was short-lived. I let my rear end sink to the floor, cold as it is. I wonder just *how* cold it is, and how long we can last in here. At least we're in the cold room, not the freezer.

"So what do we do now? I wish I could remember how we got here." I'm back to talking to Kevin—surprisingly enough, it's better than nothing.

"You know how we got here." That condescending look again.

"No, I don't. Are you telling me *you* know?"

"Well, we certainly know where we were last."

"No, Kevin. We don't know. Or at least, I have no idea where I was last."

"We were having free massages and facials. Russian ones."

I'm speechless. It's inconceivable to me that I'd forgotten we were lying in those cubicles, enduring the unholy ministrations of Svetlana and Husband. I fell for perks from the Fit and Rural crowd? My mother always told me nothing's free in this life.

"Those facials, Kevin. The last thing I remember is having that stuff smoothed over my nose and mouth, and it smelled like ether."

"They were perfectly nice to us before you started kicking Svetlana, Ruby. Remember? You caused a holy racket and her husband had to come around the divider sheet and quiet you down."

"It wasn't me, you idiot, it was her. She was doing the screaming and yelling. I told her not to massage my toes."

"You made her do it. I'm a witness. And now look at us."

I ignore him and save my strength for the cold. The main thing is, he's made me remember—now maybe I can start putting things together.

# 26

The first thing I want to do, aside from praying for warmth, is to figure out what day it is. The place seems awfully quiet, but for all I know, it's soundproof. I don't remember noticing one way or another when I was in here last. Thanks to Kevin's memory of our massages, I know that my last conscious moment was in late afternoon on a Tuesday. I'm not feeling faint from hunger, so maybe it's still Tuesday. And my bones haven't frozen solid yet, so I'm betting this is Tuesday evening, and that we haven't been locked in here for too long. I remember no kitchen noises, which means we must have been knocked out during the dinner hour. Or maybe we were kept in another place until the kitchen staff left, and just recently brought in here.

I can't see very much anymore through the glass window—there's a faint sense of the kitchen adjacent to the cold room, but the light is dim. Now that I know the door is locked, the second most pressing priority is finding the light switch so someone can see in here if they pass by. *When* they pass by. I can't allow myself to get negative at this point—Kevin's already descended into enough depressed zombiism to cover both of us.

"Kevin, can you help? I can't do this all by myself."

"Do what?"

He's got me there. "I know I can get us out of here if you'll make an effort."

I get an empty stare. He doesn't look so good, but I don't think I'd better tell him that. Actually, he hasn't looked so good for a while now.

"Are you losing weight, Kevin?"

To my surprise, that gets a smile out of him.

"Did you notice? I thought it was about time someone noticed besides Angel."

"Well, yeah, I guess I did notice."

"I've lost over ten pounds in two weeks."

"Huh?" That's awfully fast—no wonder he looks drawn.

"You're not on the coffee and banana diet, are you? It can kill you."

"I'm on something perfectly safe and natural."

"Do you think you have first-stage diabetes?"

"Quit it, Ruby."

He's right, of course. I have more immediate problems.

Kevin promises to keep banging on the door, while I try to explore each of the four walls at arm level, looking for the light switch so someone can see us. After piercing a fingertip and tearing three of my nails on unspecified objects in my way, I finally feel the light switch along the second wall. It doesn't work. Someone must really have planned this carefully.

Okay, now what? I start feeling blindly along all the shelves I can reach. I guess the likelihood of finding a flashlight is zilch, the way my luck's going, but I don't have many choices. Behind one of the cartons on the fourth wall, I come across a small book of matches—I can hardly believe it.

"Kevin, I've found some matches!"

He's as excited as I am. "Maybe we can warm our hands with them."

"As a side effect, maybe, but I want to keep these going as long as possible. Let's see if we can smash one of the wooden crates."

This is easier said than done—in fact, we can't do it. But it does give me an idea, and I feel for a chair I remember seeing in the room last time I was here. Let's just hope it was wood and not metal.

"Found it," I yell to Kevin, and proceed to smash *it* against the wall instead of the crate. The chair is a lot flimsier, and I manage to break off one of the legs in no time. I get Kevin to crumple some packing paper around the leg and hold it there while I try to light it with one of the matches. My worry is that somehow I'll catch the whole place on fire, although I'm not sure a refrigerated room *can* burn. I think of those TV shows where they hold a flame up to the sprinkler system, but it sounds too complicated. Just for openers, I don't know if they have one here, don't know where it might be, and don't have a ladder to get up there. We'd better work with what we have.

"So what exactly are we trying to do?" Kevin seems more cooperative now.

"Well, first I want to make sure the matches last, and the torch will help with that. But I want us to do this over by the glass wall, so maybe someone will see us."

We take our booty over to the wall and light the paper there. We're incredibly lucky, because the paper gets hot enough to ignite some of the varnish on the chair leg. We've got our torch. I just hope it lasts long enough for someone to see it, and that the oxygen in the room doesn't run out. In the meantime, we're both willing to get singed just trying to get close to the fire. I can feel the warmth of it on my hands—it's heaven.

"You've got to keep banging, Kevin, while the torch is lit."

"I'm tired of banging, and I need to warm my hands some more."

I could bang on the door myself, but I'm afraid to let Kevin handle the torch—it's too precious right now.

"People know we were here—they're bound to come looking for us," I tell him. Of course, I don't add that the people who knew we were here are probably the same people who did this to us. "Give it another try."

He warms his hands, then balls them into fists and gives

a boxer's rat-a-tat to the door, while I stand there waving the torch back and forth.

I hear a faint cry.

"Do you hear that, Kevin, or am I imagining it?" I wave furiously.

The sound's getting nearer now.

"Fire! Fire!"

"Someone's yelling *fire,* Kevin. I hear it!"

In a burst of faith now that someone's heard us, I give him the torch to wave and I start banging on the door myself.

No wonder Kevin didn't want to do this—it's hard. I'm exhausted after just a few bangs, and I'm trying to absorb how it feels when my hands are suddenly warm from the fire and the activity, but the arms they're attached to are still like ice. As are all my other body parts, of course.

"This torch is burning down," he says.

Just as I'm headed toward the matches to light another chair leg, there's a slam on the door from the other side. Two maintenance men and one of the reception staff blast into the room and almost knock over Kevin and his waning torch. We both drop everything and run out into the hall toward the warm air. Then we collapse in a heap.

"We called the fire department," they tell us—not reassured by the fact that the torch is already going out.

We make quite a sight in our reverse snugglies—Kevin bursting out of his pale pink sweat suit and me draped in sagging royal blue. The part of my mind that's not too tired to react is wondering why these people aren't spreading on the TLC—I think our escape was quite heroic. I find out why when the fire department arrives, accompanied by the police.

Forget the accolades. Kevin and I are put in handcuffs, dragged out into a waiting van, and hauled away to the police station.

"Hey, what's going on?" he yells as we drive off.

"You're being arrested, mister. For trying to set the place on fire."

# 27

Repeating Lieutenant Paul Lundy's name like a mantra seems to be getting me nowhere fast. I start with the guys driving the paddy wagon, continue with the desk sergeant at the station, and end up begging the woman inking my fingers to please, please call Lieutenant Lundy. Lawyers they'll get me, but I see no reason to bring a lawyer into this farce until I've spoken with Paul—though I'm not looking forward to his reaction.

Meanwhile, our pink and blue reverse Bobbsey Twins act is drawing a good deal of attention among the rank and file—they don't know what to make of us. My own opinion, which counts for zilch, is that we're pretty sorry arsonists, even though we *were* caught with a flaming torch.

I finally see a maintenance man who appears to recognize me—he gives a little grin and waves as he's mopping. I remember saying *hi* to him last time I visited the station.

"Can you possibly call Paul Lundy for me before they bring out the firing squad?" I try to yell discreetly across the room.

"No, but I can find somebody who will," he says, and disappears into the back office. I'm so grateful I could run over and kiss this guy. Leave it to the lowest man on the totem pole to take a chance on calling Lundy—the rest of this gang has obviously decided we weirdos aren't worth risking the wrath of an officer so high on the food chain.

Kevin's watching all this hyperactivity on my part with an alarming lack of interest—he's totally spaced-out, looking at me with glazed eyes as he perches uncomfortably on the edge of one of the metal folding chairs. Maybe he's in shock.

Just as I'm about to demand medical aid as a way of getting someone's attention, Paul comes striding through the massive front doors. I guess he's not amused. Now that I realize why no one was dying to drag him in from off duty, I'm even more grateful for that maintenance guy's help. Which only goes to prove my credo that if you want something done, ask the person with the least to lose.

I might have the advantage, though, because Paul's obviously thrown off his stride by our appearance.

"What is this, *Romper Room?* Are you two in your jammies?"

"No, we're in coordinated sweat suits from the Fit and Rural spa. They just got a little mixed up while we were rendered unconscious during our massages. Before we were locked in the cold room and had to get out by setting the chair legs on fire."

If you can't lick 'em, shock 'em.

I succeed.

"Okay, Ruby, I surrender. Get your tushes in my office, pronto."

First I get him to tell us what day it is—Tuesday, like I thought, about ten o'clock in the evening. Then I make sure Kevin's comfortable in the larger chair, and I pour out the whole story, starting with Svetlana and Husband, and ending with the arson accusations in the paddy wagon.

"So you can see," I say, heading him off, "that I was doing nothing—absolutely nothing in the way of what you so politely call *overreaching,* to cause this state of affairs. All we were doing was getting a free massage."

"I agree you didn't cause this, but you *have* been seen hanging around that freezer area twice now. Do you think someone wanted to kill you?"

"Hey, you're the cop—remember? How do I know? And how about Kevin?"

"It sounds rather extreme, to do both of you in. You're too well known. Especially the rabbi."

At the mention of his name, the rabbi looks up dully, scratches under the arm of his pink Dr. Denton's, and hiccups.

"People in shock often hiccup," I remind Paul.

"Ruby, where do you come up with these little hints from Heloise?"

"It's true. I read it in *Prevention* magazine. Or possibly *Consumer Reports*. I don't like Kevin's pallor."

"Maybe pink isn't his color. Do you have anything to add, Rabbi? And do you feel sick? Can I get you some water?"

"No, I'm fine."

Just like Kevin. He'd die before he'd admit I was right about something. Even his voice sounds stronger now that Paul's interrogating him.

"How about Ruby's account of what happened?"

"It's okay." Kevin seems to have acquired a second wind, but he can't scrape up quite enough energy to contradict me.

"If Kevin's fine, what do you want us to do now, Paul? I have some ideas."

"I'm sure you do, but now that I have a full report, leave it to me. Go home and warm up with some hot toddies. We'll drive you."

I'm not quite ready to go. "Are you going to unbook us? And is that legal?"

"I'll take care of it."

"How about the fingerprints?" Kevin chimes in.

"I'll take care of it."

"One other thing, Paul. I'm not leaving until you at least try to locate those Russian masseuses. No one else was around, so they're the key to this mess."

"All right, I'll make a call and see if I can get a statement from them. You can wait in case I need you for clarification."

"Oh, there's no question you'll need clarification. Their *English* is atrocious."

"Great. Just what I need to make my night off complete."

He picks up the phone and we listen while he goes through the main operator, to the staff person on duty, to the night manager on duty, and finally to Harmon Poundburn, who's burning the midnight oil overseeing the cleanup of the mess we made in the cold room. I can't believe what I'm hearing. Or at least one side of what I'm hearing. Finally, Paul finishes the call and hangs up, first asking that the staff be assembled for questioning tomorrow morning at Fit and Rural.

"Well, you heard it," he says as he stands up. "I don't need you for clarification because there are no Russians."

"What do you mean, there are no Russians?" I say. "They're lying."

"So do *you* two want to file charges? I'd planned to spend the rest of tonight getting you 'unbooked' as you called it, but I can work two tracks at once if necessary."

"No, I'm too tired and confused to do anything else right now," I say. "Find those masseuses."

Kevin's just now absorbing it all. "No Russians?" he repeats.

"Just what I said, Rabbi. There are no Russian masseuses on the staff. No one's ever heard of them."

"That's impossible," Kevin says. "Ruby and I both had massages from them. We're witnesses."

Kevin's getting agitated, and I watch his face go from beet red to an ashen white. He crosses the threshold of Paul's office and heads toward the front desk, but he never makes it. Instead, he crashes over in a pink heap.

# 28

When I walk into Kevin's hospital room today, he's getting more attention than I'd wish on my worst enemy. Essie Sue's holding his hand on one side of the bed, while Angel supports his other hand, which is attached to a precariously balanced IV bottle. It's leaning dangerously leeward as a result of her ministrations, but no one seems to notice.

"I don't believe in IV treatments," she tells me in lieu of a hello, "but they've promised me that nothing chemical is entering his body. It's basically Gatorade."

Reassured by that nutritional update, I ask Kevin how he's feeling this morning.

"He's bad," Essie Sue answers for him, "very bad. And I

wasn't notified until breakfast time today." She glares at me. "I can't believe you knew about this last night, Ruby, and didn't call me. Angel had to give me the shocking news that he'd fainted in the police station."

"Imagine how I felt as his fiancée. She didn't phone me, either." Angel's waving her arms for emphasis, which isn't helping Kevin as the needle bounces around in the vein of his hand.

My eyes are wandering toward the exit door in case I have to make a quick getaway. The angels of mercy are apparently taking no prisoners. I also notice that Kevin has yet to open his mouth.

Essie Sue's not finished. "The most embarrassing part for the community is that you allowed a respected clergyman to suffer the indignity of riding in a police van with who knows how many disgusting criminals, Ruby."

"Kevin and I went through an ordeal last night, Essie Sue, and if you don't let me speak to him, I'm calling hospital security to have you removed from the room."

She shuts up, and I know I'd better talk fast, while she's shocked into what I'm sure will be a short-lived silence. Actually, Kevin doesn't look so bad. His color is back, and he seems somewhat rested.

"I hear they performed a lot of tests last night, Kevin. They wouldn't let me stay around after midnight, but they did tell me they couldn't find any major problems."

"They said I simply passed out, Ruby. I was feeling a little queasy when we were in Lieutenant Lundy's office, but I thought it was just from all the excitement. I'm better today."

"I'm really glad, Kevin. Without our teamwork, I don't think we would have made it out of that cold room last night." Yikes. I think I've bonded with him.

"Ruby, you *know* we were on the massage tables with those Russians. How could no one have heard of them at the ranch? I keep thinking and thinking about it." He's becoming obviously upset, and tries to sit up. Essie Sue steps in front of me and grabs his hand again.

"Don't worry about it, Kevin." It's not easy to calm him. "Paul Lundy is very competent—he'll take care of it, and it's not good for you to worry about it while you're recovering."

I don't think his small room can hold one more person, but it's about to be tested. One of the hospital residents walks in, accompanied by a young woman whose badge says she's part of the laboratory staff. I try to disappear into a far corner—I'd prefer my medical updates come from someone other than Angel, and I want to stick around for any reports. Sure enough, the doctors ask Essie Sue and Angel to wait outside.

"Her, too," Essie Sue says, pointing to me.

"I was locked in the cold room with Rabbi Kapstein," I remind them, "and the doctors last night asked me to add whatever I could to your information." Not exactly what the doctors said, but close enough to give me a pass to stay.

"I want to go over some of the questions you answered in the emergency room last night, Rabbi Kapstein." The resident pulls out a clipboard with forms attached, and grabs the chair Essie Sue left at Kevin's side. "I know it was late and that they may have been filled out rather hurriedly.

"This is the medication questionnaire you filled out. You listed one allergy medication as your only prescription drug. Is that right?"

"Yes, I only take that and buffered aspirin."

"Nothing else?"

"Some seaweed powder Angel gave me, and vitamins. I forgot to say that. She's my fiancée, and she's into wellness. And other stuff."

The lab woman comes alive at this point. "Well, of course, we should all be into wellness," she says. "But when you say 'other stuff,' do you mean your fiancée is into other stuff, or that she gave you other stuff?"

Sharp. A girl after my own heart.

"Well, she gives me stuff off and on. According to what my menu is that week. Angel's very much into menu planning, supplemented by Virtual Food."

I do a double take here. "Pardon me, Kevin, but did you say Virtual Food?"

Kevin remains unperturbed. "Yeah. Angel's theory is that the food we eat is Real Food, but that because of all the pesticides in the ground, the pure distillation of vitamins that we get in a bottle is more real than Real Food. Kind of like Virtual Reality. I haven't caught on to it yet like she has, but that's the gist of it."

This rings true to me. The *gist* of it, as he puts it, just about reaches Angel's nut level.

"Angel can give you samples of what I take," Kevin says.

No way. "You're doing blood tests, right?" I ask.

"Yes, that's what we're doing." The lab woman is on my wavelength. I think.

"Kevin, do you keep all your daily vitamins in one place at home?" I'm approaching this nice and easy.

"Yes, I keep the whole selection on the kitchen windowsill so I can take them with my orange juice."

"Then I have a suggestion I'm sure the rabbi won't mind," I tell the resident. "With his permission and perhaps with the lab technician accompanying me, why don't we just run into his apartment and pick up the vitamins from the kitchen? Is that okay, Kevin?"

"I guess so. My key's under the fake plastic rock at the edge of the doormat."

Burglars beware—this fellow's gonna keep you on your toes. But hey, this is not my main concern. What I'm happiest about is that the two Enforcers are not in the room—they probably wouldn't let me get near the place. They must be *plotz*ing out there in the hall.

"As long as you don't mind having your friend do this," the resident says. "After all, we're not authorized to go into people's homes. We'd just like to confirm some of our lab results."

"Did you find something you couldn't identify?" I ask the lab woman.

She doesn't say yes and she doesn't say no. "We've sent some blood samples away for more tests. But the vitamins will make our job easier, and I'll be glad to go along with you to pick them up."

Somehow, I'd like to get a head start on Angel. I try a small ploy on the resident.

"The rabbi looks awfully tired, and his two other friends have been here quite a while. Forgive the suggestion from a civilian, but do you think maybe he ought to rest? They can be pretty talkative." I give my best conspiratorial look, and he goes for it.

"I think that's an excellent idea. We'll put the NO VISITORS sign on the door while you take a nap, Rabbi."

I say good-bye and race outside just ahead of the resident, and not a minute too soon. Angel and Essie Sue are so close to the door I almost knock them over, which is what I figured. I'm glad hospital doors are so heavy and thick—they obviously haven't heard anything. As I'm barring the door, the resident puts up the NO VISITORS sign.

"Oh my God, what's happened?" Essie Sue is panicking.

"He's fine, just very tired," the resident says, while the lab tech starts down the hall with me. "You'll both have to come back and visit later."

"Are you sure?" Angel asks.

"Very sure."

Since the resident is so efficiently doing my work for me, I decide this is the perfect chance to make a break for it without staying around for any interrogations. If I'm lucky, we'll have come and gone from Kevin's apartment before Angel and Essie Sue hear the story from him.

# 29

We find the hidden key much too quickly for Kevin's good, and let ourselves into his "bachelor" pad with no trouble. I expect to see lots of books lining the walls, but either they're still packed away, or our rabbi's not a book person. What he is, though, is a fitness buff. I see within the space of the small living room, six different pieces of equipment—a reclining and an upright exercise bike, one huge ski machine, two stair steppers, and a Thighmaster. And I take it back about no books—scattered on the floor between machines are two Weight Watchers cookbooks—one for complete meals and one for quickies.

There are no pictures on the walls yet—just bare

expanses of white. The lab tech, who's now introduced herself to me as Jean Edwards, seems as disoriented as I am—we have no place to stand, much less to sit.

"I wonder where he lives?" Jean's rolling her eyes. "The place looks like a retail outlet."

"Maybe in the bedroom," I say, pointing to the only other room in the apartment besides the kitchenette. We look at each other—mutually deciding our mission doesn't include invading Kevin's bedroom, and head for the tiny kitchen.

"He said the vitamins are on the windowsill," Jean reminds me, and sure enough, there's a double line of bottles taking up the whole sill. I count sixteen—enough to choke a horse. Jean scoops them into a leather carryall, and we look around to see what, if anything, to do next.

"I guess we're all set," I say, tripping over the reclining bike on my way to the front door. I grab the handlebars for balance, and see a tag attached.

PROPERTY OF ESSIE SUE MARGOLIS, it reads.

Aha—now it all makes sense. Essie Sue's unloaded all her old models on Kevin, and obviously, he hasn't been able to say no. Jean says she remembers Essie Sue, so I don't have to explain further.

"I'll bet the cookbooks are hers, too," she says.

"Oh, yeah, the woman *really* wants Kevin to lose weight. He's not so heavy, but that hasn't stopped her."

We're about to leave, when Jean asks me to wait.

"I want to check the kitchen and bathroom wastebaskets," she says, "an old holdover from the days I used to work in the medical examiner's office."

"I can't imagine there's anything criminal about the

rabbi," I say, "unless it's his unwholesome alliance with Essie Sue. I have to admit I'm not exactly one of his fans, but he did seem cooperative about letting us in here."

"Why shouldn't he be? We're conducting this little investigation for the benefit of the man's health, aren't we?"

I guess I've put her on the defensive, but the idea of the wastebasket search seems a bit extreme to me.

"I found an empty pill bottle with no label in this kitchen step-on can, so I'm throwing it in with the rest of the stuff," she says.

I don't respond this time. Actually, I like Jean. It's refreshing to meet someone who's unapologetically attached to her job.

We pick our way around the heavy equipment and get out of there, remembering to put the key back under the fake rock at the door. Now that we have all the pills safely in hand, I'm curious about two things. Are all the pills kosher, so to speak, and how will Kevin's giving us permission to visit his apartment go down with Essie Sue and Angel? Essie Sue hasn't mentioned a word to me about her complimentary fitness decor for Kevin's living room—I can see why. Maybe if I'd known, I could at least have shaved the count from six machines to one or two. I wonder if he has to report in on the daily usage.

I don't have to wait long for a reaction. I drop Jean at her second-floor lab and get off the elevator at the sixth floor, where Kevin's ensconced. The NO VISITORS sign has been removed from the door, so I walk in. Kevin's looking worse than ever, thanks I'm sure to the haranguing that's going on from both sides of the bed.

"What do you mean you gave Ruby permission to go to your apartment?" That's Angel, apparently not caring if the Universe is within hearing distance—she's plainly pissed. "The apartment is *our* place—we're engaged. Didn't you think of our privacy?"

"But, Angel honey, you never even come to my apartment—you said there's no room."

Truer words were never spoken. I can't see Angel manipulating her way through the aerobics maze.

"He's not in his right mind, Angel. Can't you understand these hospital drugs have weakened him?" I see Kevin wince—Essie Sue's jiggling his IV arm again to emphasize her point. I've waited long enough.

"Okay, guys, here I am. Why not give Kevin a break and accost me for a while? And please, please, Essie Sue, give the man back his arm."

They both drop his arms and turn toward me. I'm not sorry I've startled them—maybe they'll be less inhibited. If this pair can get any less inhibited.

"One at a time, ladies. I'll call on you first, Angel." Surprisingly, they're waiting their turns.

"How can you take advantage of my fiancé like that, Ruby?"

"Angel, why are you getting so excited over vitamins, of all things?"

I've rarely seen her so flustered.

"Because you're obviously trying to blame Kevin's illness on the supplements I've advised him to take."

She's got a point.

"I didn't cause the hospital staff to question what he's

ingested—they did that all by themselves. They took a blood sample, Angel, and they're trying to match what they found."

"What *did* they find?" Essie Sue, as usual, is bottom-lining it.

"I have no idea. I was just helping the lab tech gather some samples. It's not as if we broke in—although considering your fiancé's security system, that would have been easy enough."

"These are the same supplements we use at Fit and Rural, and I was just trying to add some extra nourishment to Kevin's food plan."

"Then maybe we should check with Fit and Rural."

To say the color is draining from Angel's face as we speak would be an understatement—I haven't seen her like this since that time she visited my house and I asked her to talk about Bogie.

"I did this on my own—they have nothing to do with it."

"Okay, calm down. What I can't understand, Angel, is why you're more upset about some vitamins than about our being locked in a refrigerated room last night, after we'd had massages from two of your employees who now appear to be nonexistent."

"I'm sure all that will be straightened out. I think you and Essie Sue should leave now and let Kevin and me be alone for a while."

"How about it, Essie Sue? Shall we give the lovebirds some privacy?" I'm sure Angel has closed down for the short term, at least, and it's time to pry Essie Sue away—

especially now that she's back in her position at Kevin's right hand.

"Trust me—the IV operates by the law of gravity, Essie Sue, you don't have to jiggle the Gatorade down the tube."

# 30

E-mail from: Ruby
To: Nan
Subject: *Quit Worrying*

Yeah, it *was* scary in the cold room, but it's over, and the police are investigating. What I want to know is how the Russians landed, and why no one knows about them. I'm going back to the spa because now the cops are all over the place, and it's the perfect time for me to be ever-present there. Especially since I have plenty to research all of a sudden. And I'm not pressing charges against Fit and Rural yet, because then I wouldn't be able to wander at will.

Most of the lab tests came back, and the vitamins Kevin was taking were just that—vitamins. Sixteen varieties, I admit, but they haven't killed him. Angel seems vastly relieved—too relieved for my taste. Jean, the lab tech, says that the empty pill bottle she found is a long shot, but she's pursuing it. I want to nose around on my own.

I've made very brief visits to Kevin so he can recover without all our hassle. He looks much, much better. His cheeks aren't so hollow, either. That could be because of the bagels and lox he's asked Milt to slip him on the sly.

E-mail from: Nan
To: Ruby
Subject: *What Will Essie Sue Think?*

Leave it to Milt to help a starving man! And speaking of starvation, please have him send me another care package. The bagels around here taste like they come from the Christian Coalition Recipe Book. Your food gifts have saved my life this year—right now my Contracts grade from Professor Cohen depends on the next shipment—he loves the onion-garlic.

I think you're nuts to hang around

that spa after all that's happened, but I don't expect to talk you out of it. Just be careful. I'd hate to lose my bagel connection.

# 31

Hetty Poundburn is actually contorting her face into what I think is a semblance of a smile as I walk into her office at Fit and Rural. This is a first. The fringes on her pink suede western vest are jiggling at me as she gets up from her desk and reaches out to shake my hand.

"I just want to say how sorry I am that you and the rabbi had trouble with those locks on the cold room door the other night. I think they might have stuck from the low temperature. And I'm real sorry our security guards didn't know who you were and called the police. They're trained to do that in an emergency."

Huh? We somehow locked *ourselves* in? And put on each

other's pink and blue sweat suits by mistake, I guess. After passing out from our massages.

"Hetty, didn't you read the police report? If not, I'll be glad to repeat the story to you, beginning with our massages in the late afternoon." It's taking all my strength to keep from telling her we might press charges, but I know I'm better off not being the enemy for now.

"Oh, I read the police report," she says. "I just think a few things got confused due to the trauma you went through. I'd be mixed up myself if a cold room door locked behind me. What can we do to make it better?"

To make it go away, she means. Dream on, lady.

"So do you think we were hallucinating the massages?"

"Well, I understand you have no coupons to show us advertising free massages that day, and no one here ever heard of the couple you described. To tell you the truth, I wish you *hadn't* imagined these people after your ordeal, because the police have been all over this place for days now, asking questions and getting our clients riled up."

The fake smile is fading fast. She's in a bind now—part of her wants to do her usual number on me, but the other part is being duly cautious. The woman might seem nuts, but she's no fool. Which, unfortunately, is true of most of the characters I've met around here. I can see I'm not going to get anywhere with Hetty, so I might as well press my one advantage.

"Hetty, you asked how you could make it better. As you can imagine, I haven't been feeling all that well since my *ordeal,* as you described it. But I need to get back to work on your computer system. I want to do some of that work at home, if it's okay with you. Lieutenant Lundy said you'd been most cooperative, and that if this continued, everything could be cleared up soon. I told him and my physician that I was sure you'd be understanding about my needing to be in a more comfortable work environment for a while. Doctor's orders, you know."

I have no idea what Lieutenant Lundy has to do with doctor's orders, but I'm throwing his name in for good measure. I know she wants to stay on his best side.

She does, but not without another thrust at me.

"I'm sure we can delay your work for a while," she says. Nope, she's no dummy.

"No, that would just cause me more agitation, Hetty. I have other things scheduled for later, and since I'm home anyway, I'd like to finish your work. Is there a problem? Maybe Lieutenant Lundy could help me explain, since I'm not really in top form today. Could you let me borrow your phone?"

She whips her hand out to catch me at the wrist as I'm reaching for the telephone. "Just do it," she says, "and get the files back here as soon as possible."

"Thanks," I say over my shoulder as I'm halfway out the room. Luckily, her permission was nice and general. So I'm interpreting this as a license to take the hard copies *and* the computer disks.

I'd love to get down to the basement and back out again without running into anyone else in management. I figure it'll take me two trips to lug the stuff to the car, and I've brought along a set of luggage wheels in the trunk to help out.

I'm dashing out to the parking lot when I run smack into Ardis—I'm just glad it's not Angel. Angel's becoming entirely too intrusive since she's become the rabbi's almost-wife.

Ardis looks smashingly out of place, as usual. Or maybe it's Hetty who's out of place with the rich clientele—I'm not sure which. When I'm smart enough to figure that out, I'll be a lot less perplexed about this spalike, ranchlike oddity amid the cornfields.

"Hello, Ruby, dear. How are you feeling?"

"Not great, Ardis. I'd love to talk to you about our experience sometime. Right now, I'm in a rush."

Since I know she spends her whole life in a rush to do lunch, or do meetings, or whatever else she does there, this should sound normal.

"So where are you off to?"

I have to regroup, since I'm not exactly *off* yet. I have a couple of cartons of computer equipment in the trunk, which I suppose I'll have to haul out for effect. Better still, I'll leave the spare equipment in the spa basement and put the files in the same boxes. In the general bustle, I doubt anyone will be able to figure out what I'm hauling away.

"I'm getting some stuff out of the trunk that I need for my work," I say, hoping I sound more casual than I'm feeling. I *really* don't want to tell her I'm taking the files home.

"Do you need one of the men to help you?"

"No, I have a wheel set. Thanks."

I thought she'd leave, but she's standing there, so I guess I have to go into my act. I lift up the trunk, take the wheel set out, put one of the cartons on the folding platform, and then distractedly shake the dust off an old tarp, waving it her way.

Eureka—like magic, Ardis disappears into her Lexus a few seconds ahead of the dust particles. I know my customers.

It takes longer than I expected to load and unload the boxes, but I complete the job without running into anyone but some maintenance men, who are happy to look the other way where work is concerned.

My mission is to comb those files until I come up with some reason why this so-called health spa is so attractive to people who look like they belong at the Golden Door, not the Rusty Gate.

Something's not kosher, and I don't mean Essie Sue's matzo balls.

# 32

Oy Vay's stretched out over some of the file folders I've carefully sorted by date in rows covering my living room floor. I'm good at this, and it gives me a certain perverse satisfaction to search for something out of nothing—a gold nugget from all this dross. Even Oy Vay is careful not to disturb the order—when she stirs at all, her three legs move in delicate cat-style instead of dog fashion—picking her spots whenever she resettles.

Searches are more subtle when you don't know what you're looking for. The solution can come through an emerging pattern, or from a random, isolated event that keeps bobbing to the surface. What's nagging at me after a couple of hours with these files is a rather ordinary resignation letter sent to the Poundburns two months ago.

*Dear Sirs,*

*Please accept my resignation as a staff member of your Wellness Care Section, effective at the end of this week. I realize that you may require more notice, but I have the opportunity to take up a new position across the country where I am needed ASAP, so I am requesting that you grant me this consideration. If I do not hear otherwise, I will assume I can collect my last paycheck this Friday. My new position will be of a more clerical nature, since I have learned that it is best for my emotional well-being not to become so attached to the individuals in my care.*

*Sincerely yours,*
*Gert Rae Anderson*

What in the hell is the Wellness Care Section? I never heard of it, and I don't see it mentioned anywhere—not that this means much, since Fit and Rural's organizational structure is practically nonexistent. For example, I still have no idea whether Ardis, the Poundburns, or even Angel and the PR guy, Sonny Maples, are on different organizational levels. I'm assuming Angel and Sonny are on a lower level, although it's not clear, since I can't find the management salary schedules. But even leaving that issue aside, this Gert Rae Anderson letter pushes some buzzers—not too insistently, I admit, but still.

The woman lives, or lived, on Twelfth Street right here in Eternal. It's odd that in the course of such a straightforward letter, she wouldn't have at least mentioned the state she's moving to, or even have asked for a reference, since she seems to have been an employee in good standing. The other thing that pokes at me is that gratuitous remark about becoming too close to her clients for her own good. That's strange—after all, it's a spa, not some sort of hospital.

Staff members on her level are usually assigned to specific clients for their entire stay at the ranch. They act as guides at first, and can be general aides during the rest of the stay, as needed. This must make tipping more efficient, too, at the session's end—clients know who's been responsible for their care. I see from Gert's worksheets that just before her resignation, she was assigned to help five clients. On the bottom of one client file—that of a Mr. Peter Dolby—is the word *deceased,* written in pencil. Since I suppose plenty of these people are over sixty and trying to stay healthy, this is no huge surprise. There's no indication that he died here—only that he's now deceased. And yeah, I see from the records that he was fifty-nine. Not exactly ancient, either.

If I had even one friend on the staff at the ranch, I'd try to nose around personally. But the truth is, I don't. I'm nice to all the workers, but there isn't one of them I'd trust not to report to someone that I was too curious. This is just a peculiar bunch, and after the latest fiasco near the freezer, people are even more wary of me at the same time that they're being extra solicitous.

On a whim, I pick up the phone and call the old number that's listed on the employment form. When a woman answers, I say, "Gert?"

She automatically answers, "Yes," and just as quickly changes her tone.

"Who is this?" she asks.

I think fast and say, "I'm selling . . .," and sure enough, she hangs up. If I'm lucky, she'll forget all about it.

Okay. All we know so far is that this Gert didn't go ASAP all the way across the country for a job, since she resigned a couple of months ago. Anything could have happened, of course, with her new position. If it fell through, though, she certainly didn't return to the ranch. But she's already given a reason for that—she wants a different kind of job. This isn't a great lead, but it's all I have.

I put Oy Vay in the backyard—she's not *that* trustworthy—and leave all the folders on the floor. If this trip turns out to be a flop, I'll come right back home and keep on paper-shuffling. There's a good side and a bad side to running over to Twelfth Street right this minute. I know she's home, and that's no small advantage. The disadvantage, of course, is that if she thinks about it, she'll connect the visit to the phone call I just made, and she'll refuse to see me. I'll worry about the downside when the time comes.

It comes in about ten minutes—this is a small town. I ring the bell of a tiny, wooden frame duplex on a residential street containing inexpensive rental housing. I should say, it *used* to be inexpensive housing—I'm sure now that Eternal's gone from small-town-south-of-Austin to almost-suburb-of-Austin, the houses are worth twice what they were ten years ago.

A woman in her forties, I'd say, sticks her head out the door. Even at a glance, I can tell she has a good face—and I trust my hunches. Not that a good face means a dumb face—I'll be lucky if I can keep the head out the door long enough to convince her to let me in. Hell, I wouldn't let *myself* in, so why should she?

I decide my best and probably only bet is to fling words out that she's not expecting, and to do it fast.

"I've come on behalf of Peter Dolby, deceased," I say. "I know you were concerned about him when he was in the Wellness Care Section of Fit and Rural."

Her face pales, but she lets go her grip on the doorknob a bit. If I *were* selling something, this would be the time to put my foot in the door, but I haven't stooped that low yet. Besides, I don't think that approach would do much good with this lady.

"Are you a family member?" she asks.

"No, ma'am, I'm working on some client files. We noticed that according to a penciled-in addition to the files, Mr. Dolby had died subsequent to his stay at Fit and Rural, and that you were one of his caretakers."

"Hey, I had nothing to do with his heart attack."

"Oh no, Ms. Anderson. As a matter of fact, we understand that Mr. Dolby had mentioned how grateful he was for your concern during his visit to the spa."

I'm trying not to be pinned down about exactly who it is I'm supposed to be. I haven't said I'm an investigator, and it's certainly true I'm working on some client files. At this point, I think Gert Anderson is more interested in her own role than in mine, and I hope I can keep it that way.

"I thought I had a note here in my briefcase somewhere about your interest in the clients assigned to you, but I'm having a problem balancing all this. Do you suppose I could trouble you and come inside for a minute? Do you have a table I could dump some of this stuff on?"

"I have my dining room table—I work there sometimes. I guess you can come in."

First hurdle passed. Maybe she thinks he left her something. At any rate, this invitation inside buys me some time.

The dining room table smells of lemon wax, and in fact, the whole little duplex is lustrous. The furniture's discount house, but it shines. Gert offers me tea, and I know I'm in. I just need to be careful not to blow it.

"Call me Ruby." I'm already spreading papers out on the table.

"You can call me Gert," she says, warming up, but not so much that she doesn't eye the paper spread warily.

"Look," I say, "I don't know a lot about Peter Dolby, and I guess you don't, either, after working with him only a couple of weeks, but could you tell me if you saw any signs of illness before he went home? Did he use the exercise machines like everyone else?"

"Oh yes, he was quite vigorous at first. Of course, you know he had to lose weight to avoid a heart bypass. He wanted to do it in a hurry. A lot of these people come for health reasons."

"Do their doctors send them?"

"No, I don't think so. The clients know they have health problems, and a spa seems like a good solution. We weren't working with their doctors at home, though. I would have known, because I had to make entries in their files."

"So who guides the individual programs?"

"Oh, we had very good exercise physiologists—they set up the schedules."

The one aspect of Fit and Rural I've had no experience with is what goes on in the exercise rooms, so I'm having to take her word for it about the experts. Though from what I've seen of their management *experts,* I'm not as certain as Gert seems to be.

I'm sipping my tea and trying to figure out how to broach the next subject without losing my interviewee. Something happened during the last part of Peter Dolby's session at the spa, and I'm betting it's related to Gert's leaving her job, getting too close to him—whatever. I wonder if there was an attraction there.

"Tell me about Peter Dolby." Let's see what I can get on direct examination.

"He was a lovely man—very shy. He was a widower."

"I'm a widow myself." I say, "I know how tough that can be. Did you feel he seemed interested in you?" I've found that personal questions made with no assumptions attached can often pass muster.

"Oh no, there wasn't a hint of that. Besides, there's supposed to be no fraternization between the staff and the clients."

"I didn't mean interest from your side—I just wondered if he seemed to like you. You're such a gentle person, and I imagine you were good at your job."

"I was. And sometimes a man would initiate some inappropriate behavior. But not Mr. Dolby. He was very kind, and he talked to me about his children—especially at the end of his stay, when he was resting in between activities."

"Did he rest a lot?"

"Only at the end. After they changed his vitamins. A young woman used to come in and give him a special formula capsule—all natural, she said, like the rest of the vitamins."

"Oh, I'll bet that was Angel somebody—I read in the files that was her territory."

"Yes, Angel Elkin. She was always carrying on about the transformational power of nutrition. I didn't take to her."

"Why?"

"Not my type."

I can see that, but it doesn't tell me much. I'm holding back, though, on any opinions—she undoubtedly wouldn't *take* to that. I'll have to wait her out, because I know there's something she wants to talk about.

"So did the new vitamin help him get his energy back?"

"No, I told you his energy left him *after* he took the vitamin. That whole last week, he was listless. I told Angel about it and she more or less told me it was her area and I should mind my own business. She said he was just fine, and would be even better when the vitamin took hold."

"Since he liked to talk with you, did you sense from anything he said that he was reluctant to have Angel give him a new formula?"

"Oh no—just the opposite. When he came here the first week, he didn't know anyone. Then he got friendly with the other clients, and he told me that some of the Los Angeles people advised him he should get Angel to give him this natural supplement. He asked me what I thought, and I was embarrassed, because I didn't know a thing about it, and I knew from bitter experience she certainly wasn't going to tell me."

"So what did you do?"

"I just kept putting in my reports that he didn't seem to be feeling well, and that I couldn't figure out why. But every time I looked in the file again, my reports from the day before were gone. Angel told me they were being reviewed."

"She didn't ask you to stop?"

"No, she never said to stop, though I know she'd have been relieved if I had."

I figure it's now or never.

"So when did you first think about leaving?"

"It was after Mr. Dolby got sick. I just couldn't sit around and see that man suffer and no one doing anything about it."

"You said something about his heart attack. You don't mean he had it at the spa, do you?"

"No, he was just very sick for two whole days. Finally, at my urging, they had the local doctor they use—Dr. Radner—come in and look at him, but the doctor was assured Mr. Dolby was due to go home the next day, anyway. Mr. Dolby told me the doctor requested that he be sure to see his physician in California when he got home."

"So after he went home, you made your decision to quit?"

"It didn't exactly happen that way. I put in my reports that he seemed to me to get sick after he took the new vitamin formula he'd been asking for—that was the first time I mentioned the vitamin in the report. After all, I knew he had a heart condition, and I originally thought maybe coming here and doing all the extra exercise had been bad for him. Then I started thinking about the timing of the whole thing, and the vitamin came to mind."

I want her to tell it all, so I wait, which is not exactly what I'm best at. Drinking my tea helps, but I don't let my eyes wander. I pay attention, and she seems to respond to that.

"Angel didn't like my putting the vitamins in my report. She said these were medical matters that other people should be documenting, not me. So I said that was fine, and I thought medical attention was exactly what the man needed. She said I was becoming too involved personally and I should think about that."

"So did she more or less force your resignation?"

"No, I wouldn't say that. She avoided me after our conversation, as a matter of fact. It was when I heard later—via the staff grapevine—about Mr. Dolby's death, that I decided to quit. She was right—I *did* get personally involved, and I decided I'd be better off with regular office work. I wrote in my letter that I had another job because I didn't want anyone calling and talking me into staying—not that I thought they would, but just in case."

"In the file here it says you told them you were moving across the country. If you pretty much agreed with Angel's assessment of the way you handled your job, how come you wrote that? Just to be rid of them, maybe?"

"What's wrong with my saying I was moving far away?"

"Oh, I don't know exactly—it just sounded to me as if you didn't want them to be able to locate you."

She looks at me over her teacup. I know she's hesitating because I've touched a sore spot, so I take a chance.

"Gert, were you scared of them?"

I get an instant answer.

"No, of course not—it was just a job, and I've had plenty of them. I told you, they didn't harangue me. This Angel, she's not frightening, just annoying."

My take exactly. Still.

I've heard counselors say that their most revealing client comments often come at the end of a session, in contradiction to the whole thrust of a previous exchange. Gert pulls the same about-face on me.

She gets up and says, "Well, that's the end of it."

Then she adds, "There was something not kosher about the whole damn thing. First they say he's just getting used to the new vitamin and nothing's wrong with him, then he's all of a sudden so sick they have to hurry him out of there. One minute they're not calling a doctor, then the next minute he needs more doctors than they can provide."

"And when he died?" I ask.

"When I heard he died, I thought I'd better get the hell out of there and let 'em think I was a million miles away."

# 33

Oy Vay's glad to come in the house and help me pick through more of the client files. I don't feel exactly elated after my visit to Gert Anderson, who, like me, has vague suspicions but nothing solid to back them up. It occurs to me that this Fit and Rural outfit is too hokey to pin down, making the quest I'm on feel less like Don Quixote and more like Donald Duck. The clowns who run the place seem, as Gert pointed out, annoying rather than dangerous. Yet, within a short period of time, serious things continue to happen. Peter Dolby takes pills and dies, a personal trainer who's angling for a bigger job there is killed near a baseball machine, and Kevin and I are locked in a cold room. The first event seems the most tenuous, yet it pulls at me.

Gert mentioned a Dr. Radner—a physician the spa called in to examine Peter Dolby before he went back to California. On a hunch, I pick up the phone and call Radner's office. The receptionist takes the usual message, but when I tell her I'm an employee of Fit and Rural—something I'm sure I'll be sorry for later but don't intend to worry about now—she says he's in and will take the call.

"Dr. Radner, I'll just take a minute of your time. I work for Fit and Rural."

"Yes, do you need me to make a visit?" I guess he has some sort of on-call arrangement with them.

"No, I'm trying to update some important files and needed some quick information from you. I've noted that you wisely advised one of the clients, Peter Dolby, to see his physician in San Francisco as soon as he got home, to check on his condition. Did you happen to forward any files to that doctor from Mr. Dolby's stay at the spa? You seemed to be doing a very thorough referral on the patient, so I thought I'd ask."

"Yes, and I got a report back from the San Francisco physician after Mr. Dolby died, too. Why do you need to double-check? I already sent the report in to Harmon."

"Because it's not in the files I'm working from, and I want to make a notation that you did the referral and got a reply." I hope I sound halfway knowledgeable, but I always figure the briefer the explanation, the better—especially when I don't know what I'm talking about.

"His doctor confirmed to me that Dolby died of a heart attack following his return."

"Was an autopsy done?"

"I doubt it. His symptoms were consistent with the disease he was being treated for."

"Did he experience a rapid weight loss at our facility?"

"Yes, but that's what he came for. It wasn't an unhealthy loss, considering his change of diet and exercise."

"Could any of his medications have made him ill?"

"Well, considering that the man died, I guess the meds he had been prescribed couldn't hold in check the heart damage he'd already suffered."

"What about anything he was prescribed here?"

"You mean those vitamin supplements? Harmless. I don't put any stock in them myself, but they certainly couldn't have hurt him. Besides those, he wasn't prescribed anything here. Is this all?"

"Yes, Dr. Radner—thanks so much for allowing me to make these final notations before I close the file. Just routine."

Let's hope I used the word *routine* enough to make him forget the whole conversation next time he sees Harmon.

No autopsy, so there's a chance something was missed, but a slim one. I had high hopes for Peter Dolby. Now that I've done all I can do about Dolby, I'm going to follow another lead Gert hinted at—those Los Angeles clients who talked Dolby into taking the fast-weight-loss supplement. If, as Dr. Radner thinks, the vitamins are harmless, then all of Angel's ministrations are as spacey as she is, and her vitamins are no more responsible for weight loss than the mantras she has these people chanting. In other words, the usual for her. If, on the other hand, this pill *is* some hotshot fat remover, surely the clients have to pay for it. And their financial records should show it.

I decide to search through the accounts of anyone from Los Angeles who was a guest of the spa during the time spent there by Peter Dolby. It helps with the Los Angeles part that the more recent accounts are also on disk. When I finish with my job of updating the entire system, everything will be as accessible as these new records—but who knows when that will be? Meanwhile, I'm grateful to be able to pull up all the L.A. files and look at them in sequence, double-checking by confirming the hard copy. I learned a long time ago that what's put on paper is not always duplicated on the computer—people have a tendency to summarize for the electronic medium, while jotting all sorts of notes and addenda on paper.

I recognize several names from TV and movie production—I guess these are some of the celebrities the staff talks about. A couple of John and Jane Does, too—with bills sent directly to CPA firms—maybe they're movie stars or politicians. All the invoices are uniformly high—the only thing that surprises me is that people will travel *here,* to the Poundburns, to pay those prices. The charges are all on a level with Dolby's. I get a sinking feeling this is gonna be a wasted day.

"So what's the deal, Oy Vay?" She comes over to be patted, though I'm the one who needs the comforting right now, and she lets me hug her. Those moist brown eyes don't miss a trick—too bad she can't talk to me. One of her three legs lands on a pile of recent files I've put aside because they *aren't* California accounts. The stack falls over—even Oy Vay's not perfect, though she usually doesn't make a mess. I'm straightening up the pile and vaguely glancing at the columns of figures when I realize I need to look at some of these as a control group, since according to Gert, Dolby learned about the special pills from the Los Angeles people.

What I find is a puzzle—the totals for client visits on most of these sheets are uniformly lower than the ones from California, even for the same length of stay. I look at the room and meal charges—all thrown in together—and they're the same as the others. Facials and massages—listed under *Incidentals,* are extra, but in the course of a one-week visit, these totals are about the same wherever I encounter them. The overall *Incidentals* changes, though, vary tremendously. Under an incidental category called *Supplies, Supplements, Extra Products,* charges for the L.A. accounts are up to a thousand dollars more than the other invoices.

I'm hitting pay dirt here. I do a quick computer search and find that it's not just California accounts that are higher, but several of the accounts from the West Coast and Sunbelt states, as well as a few from New York. All of these raised totals come from higher figures in the *Incidentals* category.

I give Oy Vay a Milk-Bone and grind myself a pot of mocha Java—kept for very special occasions. Paul Lundy always tells me the best yields come from pure shitwork. He's right.

# 34

"I want you all to close your eyes and pretend you're my clients at a Chicago wedding in the Drake Hotel."

This is Ardis's way of summoning Nirvana, and we all try to comply—with the exception of Essie Sue, who continues to balk at her unfamiliar role as a mere planet orbiting Ardis's sun. Our task is made even harder by the fact that we're sitting on metal folding chairs in the middle of the community room at Essie Sue's Center for Bodily Movement, under a harsh fluorescent glare far removed from the Drake's crystal chandeliers.

"Rabbi and Angel, welcome to the best that my bridal service extraordinaire has to offer. Yours truly will help you achieve your highest matrimonial dreams with a minimum of planning."

Kevin and Angel, decked out in matching complimentary tee shirts reading WEDDINGS ANONYMOUS: WE TIE PERMANENT KNOTS, occupy two folding seats in the center of the room, surrounded in semicircular symmetry by those of us Ardis refers to as Bliss Assistants—draftees, for the most part. There's me, Milt, who's helping with the catering, and Kay Brown—former organist at the Methodist church—who, by mere chance of fortune, just converted to Judaism and is now deemed eligible by Essie Sue to tickle the temple ivories for a rabbinical wedding. Essie Sue, not exactly a draftee since she's the one who hired Ardis as a special wedding gift to Kevin, is the self-appointed checks and balances consultant—which means she gets to put a damper on anything Ardis suggests. So far, though, she's met her match.

At the moment, I'm *utz*ing her about it.

"I thought you were thrilled to have a big-time wedding consultant working within a twenty-mile radius of Eternal."

"Look," she says, "if we didn't have a celebrity health ranch like Fit and Rural in the area, this woman wouldn't even be here. I thought she'd let us in on some big-city ideas to help us create the classiest wedding ever held at the Temple. Instead, she's taking over."

This from the woman who invented taking over.

"Maybe she's just giving you your money's worth," I say. "Relax and enjoy it like Kevin and Angel seem to be doing."

Kevin seems to have made a miraculous recovery. He's put on a bit of weight and doesn't have those sunken cheeks anymore, and his color's back. I just hope he's up for this extravaganza. Ardis is planning a huge bash, with the whole congregation invited to the wedding and reception.

The topic of the moment is Angel's dress.

"I want my dress to be spiritual, Ardis."

"Angel, dear, just because you're spiritual director doesn't mean you need to overdo that angle. I see beaded. I see bouffant. I don't see spiritual."

"She's marrying a rabbi—I see spiritual whether you do or not." Essie Sue moves her chair into the center of the circle. Good-bye, Bliss Assistant.

"All right, we'll make the dress have a floating quality—is that spiritual enough, Essie Sue?" Wow, Ardis is yielding—that's a first.

"Next on the agenda is your remarks to each other during the ceremony," Ardis announces. "This is an engineering problem, whether you've ever stopped to think about it or not."

She's one up on me—I thought these little bride and groom exchanges were about commitment.

"Unless the space between you is effective, no one will get the significance of your speeches. I suggest to my clients that they go down the aisle together with a space between them—just picture parallel lines. Then, halfway down, you turn and look at each other and say your thing."

"Like stereophonic sound?" I ask.

"Don't be a smarty-pants, Ruby," Essie Sue says. "Listen to the woman—you may learn something."

"But don't they have to say it awfully loud?"

"No, they're wired with wireless. These are the nineties, Ruby."

I stand corrected.

"This is a specialty of mine," Ardis assures us. "It's tried-and-true, so don't worry about it. What you should worry about is what you'll say. Are you saying original or are you saying by the book?"

I shudder to think how much this *expert* is costing Essie Sue.

Angel raises her hand. "When you say by the book, is that counting quotations?"

"Of course. What else could it mean?"

"Well, what do you think, Ardis?" Angel asks. "What's most impressive?"

I take another stab at this. "Why don't you let Kevin and Angel work it out? After all, the man is a public speaker." Of sorts.

Essie Sue jumps up. "No. I'm paying for this. They should take Ardis's advice. Keep quiet, Ruby."

"I thought I was a Bliss Assistant."

"You'll come in handy later."

Yeah, when the tables need to be set up.

"My advice," Ardis says, "is that someone else's words are best. They've been tested. There are many wonderful books of quotations I can refer you to. Go buy *Blessing Ourselves: Prayer for Moderns*. I recommend it to all my clients. It has ready-made vows in it. His and hers."

"I disagree," Essie Sue says. "I like the more personalized, original remarks. Let it all hang out."

"Like a sermon," Kevin says. "Yeah, I like that."

We all glare at Essie Sue until she realizes her mistake. "Let's table that, Rabbi. We'll discuss it later."

Yeah, much later.

Essie Sue's not about to lose her advantage over one mistake. "Next item—wine. We should have Israeli wines exclusively."

"I have a deal on wines with a broker in Chicago," Ardis says. "This is business. Leave the wines up to me."

"As long as they're Israeli."

"Do you want Israeli or do you want cost-efficient? The deal is with Spain."

Kevin's all of a sudden interested. "Spain? The Inquisition? No way."

"Listen," Ardis says, "they just discovered Christopher Columbus was Jewish. You want more authentic than that?"

The gallery seems appeased, but not for long.

"I'm assuming a GE lightbulb is okay for stomping on the glass at the end of the ceremony?" Ardis is obviously trying to hurry this one through.

"This is class?"

I knew Essie Sue would have none of that. She's in full righteous mode now.

"The rabbi cannot stomp on the glass, a symbol of the destruction of the Temple in Jerusalem—for openers—with a GE lightbulb. I'm drawing the line at lightbulbs. It's a crystal goblet or nothing."

"They have very nice wineglasses at Safeway," Angel reminds us. "And it's wrapped in a napkin when he stomps, so who'll know the difference?"

"We'll know the difference. But I'll compromise—at least it's a wineglass." Essie Sue must be getting tired.

"No," Kevin says. "Those grocery store glasses are an inch thick—I'll never be able to smash it, and you know how people snicker if the groom can't even break the glass. That's why they invented lightbulbs for this in the first place. The glass in those is foolproof. You just look at it and it shatters."

No one has an answer for this, so I guess Kevin's won his point—although I doubt Edison would agree. Or GE, for that matter. It appears that Angel's none too happy, either, to hear that her groom might not crack that ever-so-important glass—although I wouldn't touch that one with a ten-foot pole.

"I have to get back to my customers, folks. I thought you were going to have a list of food for me to order." Milt's obviously had it, and he's halfway out the door.

"Oh, you're right—we haven't even started on the food," Ardis says.

"Count me out, then. You can fax me the list."

"No, we'll need your expertise." Ardis looks desperate. "We'll do the food discussion right this minute."

Essie Sue stands up for this one.

"I want the food to be Jewish in the sense of ethnic, but not too Jewish in the sense of gefilte fish balls on toothpicks, you know? I want memorable."

"Yes! I couldn't have put it better myself," Ardis says.

I look at Milt and shrug. This is the first thing Ardis and Essie Sue have agreed upon all day—I guess I should be relieved, except for the fact that the words *memorable* and *gefilte fish balls* could be compared only by the likes of these two.

"So what does this mean in terms of ordering for five hundred people?" Milt asks. "What won't pass muster on your *too Jewish* scale? I need to know before I lose all my good wholesalers over this."

"Okay," Ardis says, "I'll list the foods that are too Jewish for a really classy affair. This is not the first time I've had to do this in my career. You'd be surprised how many people need educating. This is very subtle.

"Schmaltz herring is too Jewish, but herring in wine sauce is not. Chopped liver is too Jewish in big glass bowls, but fine if it's sculpted as a swan. Little meatballs in barbecue sauce are a *yes,* but those cocktail-sized kosher wieners just seem to *announce* themselves in a way that's—*je ne sais quoi . . .*"

"Too Jewish?" Milt fills in.

"Exactly," Essie Sue says. "You're getting it. I was worried this might be complex for you as a Lebanese, Milt. Just take my word for it, you have to be Jewish to really understand."

"Oh, I think he gets it," I volunteer.

"Are we going to have anything sweet?" Kevin asks.

"Darling, you really shouldn't," Angel warns. "You're looking so handsome thinner."

"But we are having the wedding cake we talked about?" He's not giving up.

"Yes, but that doesn't count," Angel says, "so much of it is cardboard. By the time you have the filler for the shape of the Old City in Jerusalem, and then enough Styrofoam to support the little moveable bride and groom seesawing between heaven and earth, the center of the cake is pretty much taken, so to speak. And since icing has never been known for its sticking power, I told the bakery to feel free to mix in a little Elmer's glue—after all, it's white."

Ardis can't contain herself. "And really, Rabbi, what's our priority—the food value or the enduring value? I'll go for endurance every time."

Yep, that Styrofoam *will* endure—I hope they invite plenty of dentists.

"Let's tackle the music while Kay's here," Angel says. "I want a selection of songs Julie Andrews sang in *The Sound of Music.*"

"Too Waspy."

"I don't care, Essie Sue. I want *The Sound of Music.*" Angel's a teeny bit less angelic all of a sudden. She's looking at Ardis. "After all, it is my wedding. And besides, I think Julie Andrews might have been married to a Jew."

"We'll check it out, dear." Ardis takes notes.

"Thousands of Jews have been married to the accompaniment of *Fiddler on the Roof.*" Essie Sue's not giving up easily. "*Fiddler on the Roof* is to *The Sound of Music* what a good corn rye is to Wonder bread."

"How about Streisand in *Yentl?*" Kevin's calming down Angel.

"Why don't we adjourn on that note," I suggest, "and leave it to Streisand and Andrews to battle it out later?"

"There's just the little matter of the engraved napkins," Ardis says.

"Very little," I say. "This ought to be something you can handle without us."

"Oh no. I need my Bliss Assistants on this. It's one of the tenets of my profession that the cocktail napkins always match, or at the very least, coordinate with the wedding invitations. Since you ordered the invitations before you brought me into the picture, I'm now stuck with the consequences."

"Which are?"

"Isn't it obvious? The invitations are white. Plain, boring white. I haven't seen a white engraved cocktail napkin since the Reagan era, when one of my clients was planning to marry a White House intern. In that case, we went with white, naturally. But that was white with integrity. It stood for something."

"This can stand for something," I say. "It matches the Styrofoam and the Elmer's glue."

"Be quiet, Ruby—you're just trying to get out of here." Essie Sue is taking no prisoners. "We haven't sent out the invitations yet, Ardis. Why don't we seal the envelopes with stickers in a coordinating color to the napkins?"

Ardis ponders. "This could work. If the stickers and the napkins were that shrimp color we're using for Angel's makeup and for the tablecloths . . ."

Kevin perks up again. "Shrimp? Nothing doing."

"It's only a color, darling," Angel says. "It's not as if we're serving bacon Ramekins."

I've gotta get out of here because I'm having a waking nightmare where Julie, Barbra, and I are lost in the Austrian Alps with only cocktail wieners to keep us from starving—but when we bite into the tiny Hebrew Nationals, they come alive with the sound of the Israeli national anthem, which of course is too Jewish to save us.

# 35

E-mail from: Ruby
To: Nan
Subject: *Where Angels Fear to Tread*

I turned all the information I gathered from Gert Anderson over to my friend Paul, but my current dilemma is what to do about Kevin. The wedding plans are proceeding full blast, and he's tight as can be with Angel. She, on the other hand, is watchful and wary of me—not that I blame her. At this point, there's not a lot to tell Kevin—I'm not ready to let Angel know we're investigating some possible link between her and Bogie in El Paso, so I certainly can't mention it to him—he'd go right to her.

Paul asked me to give him some time to absorb the facts surrounding Peter Dolby's death. I've personally concluded Angel gave Kevin something like the pills Dolby got, and that they made him sick—not that I can prove it yet—nor would he or should he believe me *without* proof. And whatever it was, she's quit giving it to him, which can buy me some time.

You sound okay—are you set for the end of the school year?

E-mail from: Nan
To: Ruby
Subject: *Angels Don't Tread on Me*

This is unsolicited, but that never stopped me before. Did you ever ask Kevin about the pill container he threw away, or were you waiting for some lab report? Why don't you ask Lundy if you can talk to Kevin casually about it, sans police? Then you'd at least have his word for it in the face of a possible denial by Angel that she gave him anything extra.

Unless you think Kevin would cover up for her.

Am I set for the end of the school

year? There *is* no getting set for the end of the first year of law school. I'm petrified about the exams.

E-mail from: Ruby
To: Nan
Subject: *You're Right*

I decided maybe I was wrong not bringing Kevin into this—he needs to know we're concerned about what he might have ingested beyond the vitamins. Paul has given me the go-ahead to bring the empty pill container into a general conversation with Kevin and see what comes out of it, since the lab still hasn't come up with anything. As for what might happen if Kevin tells Angel, Paul said the situation is so stagnant at this point that maybe it wouldn't hurt to shake her up.

# 36

"More coffee, Rabbi?"

Milt's on his best behavior this morning, ever since I confided in him about why I asked Kevin over to The Hot Bagel for a morning snack between the breakfast regulars and the early lunch crowd. Ostensibly, we're supposed to be checking on arrangements for who'll take over while he's on his honeymoon. Essie Sue asked me to meet with him weeks ago and I turned her down, until I suddenly realized it would be a great excuse for a conversation.

"There are several rabbis looking for jobs who could take my place for a couple of weeks, Ruby."

"Oh, I don't think that'll be necessary. Why don't we

just make up a schedule of readers for services and have an Austin rabbi cover for funerals?"

What I don't find it essential to mention is that we can't afford to pay anyone else, and *he* can't afford any unnecessary competition while he's gone. I can't go through another rabbinical crisis this year, and I *have* heard rumblings.

"But who'll preach?"

"They can do without sermons while you're gone—or we could ask some of the laypeople who like to do that stuff."

"That stuff, Ruby, is not as easy as it looks—which you should certainly know from your own experience. Unless I can train someone in a hurry, I don't think that's a good idea."

"Fine, let's just have readers and forget the training. Do you want to call a few people?"

"Could you do it? I've got a lot on my mind with the wedding and all."

He always asks for that extra something, but I can't very well refuse at this point—not when I have other things on my mind. Besides, this is a good opening.

"You seem really harassed lately—I guess it's just all the excitement, and you did get out of the hospital not that long ago. Are you feeling up to par?"

"I'm fine now."

From the snack he just ate—two onion bagels with lox and cream cheese—I'd say his appetite is certainly back, but I need to keep at this.

"I didn't bother you with this in the hospital, but

remember when we went to your apartment that day to get your vitamins?"

"Yeah, Angel didn't like your trespassing."

"Did you think we were trespassing? You even told me where the key was hidden."

"She meant trespassing in a more general way—like you shouldn't have asked me."

I ignore that.

"We were looking in the wastebasket to see if there were any vitamin bottles that had just been used up and should be counted, too, and we came across an empty pill bottle that was unmarked—all the other bottles had brand names on them. Do you remember taking any other pills with the vitamins?"

"There shouldn't have been anything in the wastebasket. The maid service comes every other week, and that was their day."

"Well, I have no idea where they were, but the apartment didn't look as if they'd been there."

"They should have been. Can you check for me?"

*Oy*—he never stops. But what am I complaining about? Of course, I'll check—I'd love to know why they didn't come.

"Okay," I say. "I'll call them and see why they didn't show up. Give me the phone number." He looks in his daily planner and writes it down for me.

"But I was asking about the empty pill bottle," I say. "Any ideas?" I try to look as if I couldn't care less, and with anyone else, I probably wouldn't be bringing it off. With Kevin, I have a shot at it.

"Oh, that was probably the special one-week vitamin regimen Angel gave me. She brought over just enough pills for a week, and I was to take one a day. She said not to forget them—they were very expensive. I think the big shots at the ranch take them."

"And they were for . . .?" I'm my *most* casual now.

"Losing weight."

"Are you back on the regimen?"

"I should be, but Angel won't give me any more. I figure she probably couldn't wrangle more freebies. She says I'm taking enough vitamins at this point."

We're just beginning to warm up here, when Angel walks in. Just what we need. And this certainly can't be a coincidence—not at this time of day.

"Here comes your affianced," I say to Kevin.

"Oh, I left a message on her answering machine telling her where I'd be," he says. "We like to keep up with each other during the day. I'm surprised she'd be *here,* though—she's usually teaching classes at the ranch in the mornings."

Wish I'd thought to tell him this was confidential—at least he might have kept quiet about it until he got home tonight. I excuse myself while Angel makes her way over, and go back in the kitchen for Milt.

"Angel's here," I tell him as he's preparing some cream cheese blends for lunch.

"Yeah, I saw her," he says.

"You don't miss much, do you?"

"Not in my own store, I don't. Your store, too, of course."

"I still think of it as yours just like everybody else does, Milt—don't apologize."

"Well, you are my new partner. So what are you gonna do with Angel?"

"That's what I'm back here in the kitchen for—it never occurred to me she'd come. I could have told Kevin anything—that we were going for a ride somewhere. But I had to tell him when and where."

"You had no way of knowing. Why don't you just sit there and let it play out? He's probably telling her now everything you asked him."

"I shouldn't bring up the bottle on my own?"

"You won't have to."

"Come with me, at least."

"What's the matter with you? You're never this jumpy, Ruby."

"I just need some support. Will you come?"

"Okay. It's between shifts right now, but I'm expecting Bradley and Carol in the next fifteen minutes."

We go back over to the table, bringing some fresh bagels and coffee with us. The two lovebirds are holding hands.

"Hi, Angel," Milt says. "What brings you out?"

I wave hi with a bagel half, and get a glare in return.

"Why are you . . ." Angel stops herself in mid-sentence. I think I bring out the worst in her, and she's just realizing she needs to cool it and be civil if she's going to find out anything. At least, I *think* that's what she's thinking—maybe she's not that complex. Or that subtle.

"Are you interested in who's going to conduct the service while you two are on your honeymoon?" I ask. I'm sweet. Milt kicks me under the table and takes over.

"It's great you can take time off work to make sure the rabbi's temple business is taken care of," he says. I guess he figured I'd never get away with that one.

Angel's cornered, in a way. She knows there's no good reason for her to have dropped in, so now she's got to come up with some excuse as to why that answering machine message sent her scurrying. I decide I can relax and let *her* be uncomfortable for a change.

I gather from my reading of Milt's mind that our modus operandi is to say nothing and see what she brings up. We just sit there. I do a yum-yum over the bagel, just so our silence doesn't seem so menacing.

Finally, she can't stand it. "You're making that up about an empty pill bottle," she says. "The rabbi's cleaning service came at nine o'clock the morning you went to his apartment."

*Oy,* he's got her calling him "the rabbi" just like his ex-wife, Kitselah, did.

"They come every other week, and he's the first one on their list," she says.

"No, honey, I didn't get to tell you yet—Ruby just told me the cleaning service didn't come."

It's hard to say Angel's face actually ever pales—her skin is translucent, so she's pale all the time. But for the record—it just paled.

"Did you call to stop them?" She's looking at me. "I can check, you know."

I pull out my cell phone. "Let's do check. I've been wondering why they didn't come ever since Kevin told me."

Before she can grab the phone away from me and do it

herself, I whip out the piece of paper Kevin gave me earlier with the phone number, and dial up the cleaning service.

After five minutes of introduction, the receptionist remembers—he's the only rabbi they have on their list. She makes all the calls herself, usually at the clients' workplaces, to remind them the day before that the cleaning crew is coming. In Kevin's case, she always calls the Temple. When she did, they told her he was in the hospital, so she canceled the cleaning for that time, thinking he wouldn't want it.

I relate all this to the assembled group.

"Oh, yeah," Kevin says, "when they called for the next time, they got me at the Temple, and she probably said something about was I feeling okay. Who remembers?"

Well, obviously, not Angel. She's shrugging her shoulders, but I can bet she's not shrugging it off.

"So anyway," I say, "the bottle's being sent to all kinds of labs." The truth is, if they'd found anything, that lab tech, Jean Edwards, would have let me know by now.

"For what purpose?" Angel asks.

"For traces of some substance that might have made Kevin sick, and also for fingerprints besides his."

Angel's still cool—I've got to hand it to her. No, actually I *don't* have to hand it to her on a deli platter, so to speak. Maybe I can sneak up on her.

"It's a shame you couldn't wrangle some more of those special expensive diet pills—Kevin said they worked great."

She shoots a look at him that could coagulate hot chicken fat on the spot.

He winces. "It wasn't my fault, honey—Ruby took me by surprise. I know I wasn't supposed to tell anybody about the diet pills, but how was I supposed to know she'd go through the wastebasket? The maids were supposed to clean that."

He's digging her in even deeper than I hoped, and she's not amused. She does exactly what I'd do if I had to sit there and listen to my boyfriend spill the pills. She splits.

"I have to get back to work now." Ignoring the totality of the last few minutes, she grabs her cavernous basketweave handbag and heads out the door.

I look at Milt.

"If I were you, I'd go for it," he says. I think about it for a second, and agree with him.

"Hey, Angel! Wait up—I'm right behind you."

# 37

I start out the front door—then realize she's probably parked in the rear lot, so I go back in and race for the kitchen door. Sure enough, she's jumping into her Yugo.

Her handbag's so big it almost looks like another person in the front seat beside her. I slide into the seat and toss the purse into my lap—trying to look as normal as I can under the circumstances. She freaks, of course, and screams at me.

"Get out of here, Ruby. Are you crazy?"

"I apologize for getting in your car, Angel. But this is a police investigation now."

I keep the *this* as unspecific as possible.

"What are you talking about? I have to get back to the ranch."

"No, you don't—you took the morning off to come all the way up here to The Hot Bagel. Drive for a couple of blocks and let's park somewhere and talk. You won't be sorry—I can probably tell you a few things you didn't know. And there's a lot you can tell me."

Maybe she's curious, or maybe I'm bigger than she is—at any rate, she drives.

"How about the Wal-Mart parking lot?" she says. Eternal's first gift from the developers. Somehow it seems appropriate. And it's empty.

I'm pushing my slight advantage as we pull up to the lot. "My advice to you, Angel, is to use me as an intermediary. Lieutenant Lundy's going to want to talk to you again sooner or later, and he's a friend of mine. Why don't you tell me about it before you get officially questioned?"

She's not buying.

"Questioned about what? I've done nothing wrong. Unless you count falling in love with a man you wanted for yourself."

"You mean Bogie?"

I don't know what drives me to blurt that out, but it's inspired, and I don't say that about myself often. It has just the effect I wanted—Angel deflates immediately.

"What . . . who . . . did you say Bogie?"

"Sorry to let that slip, but you were the one being snide, Angel, about your being in love with someone I was interested in."

"But it was the rabbi I was talking about. You and he both know you were in love with him."

Ooh, she's good in the deflection department. But I smell blood.

"That's a bore, Angel. I've told you that was just Kevin's ego talking. But Bogie's another story—let's stick to that one."

*Let's stick to that one?* I said that? I have no idea where this is going. But apparently, I'm about to imply to Angel that Bogie and I were close, and that I know about their connection in El Paso years ago. This is pretty far afield from diet pills, but at this point, I can take my pick of secrets—this woman has a bushel.

"I know about you and Hubert Bogardis in El Paso. Do the Fit and Rural people know you and Bogie had a history before either of you came to the Austin area? Did you get him his job at the ranch?"

"How? How could you possibly know . . ."

Angel trails off and just slumps there, with her arms on the steering wheel to support her. "Are you saying Bogie told you?"

"I'm saying there's an open investigation into his death, and I think his death has something to do with Fit and Rural where you both worked."

The truth is that until this moment I thought the thread between Bogie and the ranch was a tenuous one, but one look at Angel tells me otherwise. She's terrified, and she takes the Fifth.

"I don't believe it," she says. "I don't believe he told you anything about us. He wouldn't."

"You were married, weren't you." This is a long shot, but if it pays off, it'll save me a lot of phone time with the El Paso hall of records.

"He couldn't have done this."

I guess I'm right. I wait until she has a chance to compose herself.

"You won't tell Kevin, will you, Ruby? It was a long time ago."

"Kevin was married before, too, Angel. Why would he be upset?"

"You wouldn't understand. It's complicated."

"I'd say it is, but if I found out, other people know, too."

I can tell her mind is skipping back and forth, alighting on all the possibilities.

"You and Bogie were involved, Ruby?"

"Not in that way, Angel. I just know about you two, that's all. Why do you want this whole mess dumped in your lap, Angel? That could be about to happen if you continue to keep it all to yourself."

The woman can't stand me, and I'm asking her to make me her confidante. It ain't gonna happen, but at least I might shake something loose.

"Let's forget about Bogie for a minute and go on to the pill question. Kevin's already said you gave him expensive pills to take for a week. Personally, I think they're what made him sick, since he's been fine ever since you told him to stop taking them. Are you really going to wait until the fingerprints and chemical evidence pile up and you're called in by the police?"

She gives me a look that says why don't you just disappear into a hole in the ground, but I can tell she's thinking about this. After all, it's her word against Kevin's at this point, and even she wouldn't be foolish enough to say he was making this up.

She leans her head back on the seat and closes her eyes. When she opens them again, she seems to have come to a decision.

"The rabbi's my fiancé. I gave him a few pills—that's all I did. You don't need to have the lab prove it—I'm telling you I gave him the bottle. But please, Ruby—please don't tell my bosses at Fit and Rural."

"Surely you wouldn't lose your job over that? They seem to like your work."

"Can't you just take my word for it that they can't know?" I see that fear pop back into her eyes. "I'm telling you, Ruby—you simply can't mention it to them. I wasn't supposed to do it."

"So blame it on Kevin. Or me, or Essie Sue—tell them we thought Kevin could benefit and we talked you into it. What's the big deal? We'll help you out."

Nothing doing. For a minute I think she's going to spill more, but she purses her mouth into a straight line as if she's physically preventing the words from escaping.

"Let's go, then," I say. "Take me back to my car." This is the psychological moment to leave—I'm sure of it. At this point, everything's left hanging. She has no idea what I'm going to do with the information, and I've promised nothing.

We're at a standoff, but now she has a chance to go back and absorb what's just happened. If she doesn't do anything, there's no doubt in my mind that someone else will.

Possibly Paul Lundy.

# 38

I'm in the fitting room of Brodman's Department Store in Austin, refusing to try on the tackiest bridesmaid's dress I've ever seen in my life.

"Thanks for meeting me here in a hurry," Essie Sue tells me. "Sorry I didn't get to tell you what this was about on the phone, but I didn't want to take the time. I know you've got a lot on your mind."

She should only know.

"Just be straight with it, Essie Sue. You didn't tell me over the phone because you knew I wouldn't come if I knew the real reason. You said it was an emergency involving Angel and Kevin."

"*Nu?* So isn't it?"

"No, it isn't. I thought something had happened to one of them when you said you couldn't leave the store unless I met you all here."

"They couldn't be here—I tried to get them to come. Kevin decided at the last minute he wanted you to be in the wedding and Ardis put me in charge of getting you outfitted. I knew it wouldn't be easy."

"You're damned right. Why aren't *you* in the wedding?"

"Why, I am, dear. I'm overseeing the whole thing—making sure our wedding consultant doesn't overdo."

Overdo? This event was overdone the day Ardis was hired, and Essie Sue's only made it worse.

"Since you're so knowledgeable about wedding protocol, Essie Sue, surely Ardis has told you that it's the bride who's supposed to pick the bridesmaids. There's no way in hell that Angel would pick me. So let's put this monstrosity back on the rack and get out of here."

"I admit it's not high fashion, Ruby, but you're not the easiest person to fit. This pale green net over taffeta was the only thing they had on short notice in your size, and the least you can do is to try it on for me."

"I can see why they had it left over. This dreck—pardon me, dress—looks like it came out of somebody's nasal passages."

"You don't have to be vulgar, Ruby. Green is a good color for auburn hair like yours."

"Not this green."

She has stopped calling me *dear*. "Listen to me, Ruby. Salmon is the coordinating color for the wedding—you know that. Ardis gave me strict instructions to look for green—what else goes with salmon? Only white, and of course, that's reserved for the bride."

This bride might well wear black for all we know—depending on who gets to her secrets first. But I do know what I'm not wearing.

"Essie Sue, you're not listening to me. Has anyone asked Angel? Call her right now so I can get out of here." I plunk down on the teeny, uncomfortable corner board they call a seat in this fitting room, and Essie Sue stands barring the door.

What's more, she's ready for me. "Who says the groom can't pick out a bridesmaid? What about sisters of grooms? Do you think the bride picks them?"

"She agrees to them. Angel thinks I'm in love with her fiancé, Essie Sue. You don't seriously think she needs me marching down the aisle in front of her?"

"We needed a bridesmaid, and you wouldn't want to see Hetty Poundburn plowing down the aisle, would you? That's Angel's social circle."

"Let me ask you something, Essie Sue. Just between the two of us—if you're already making fun of her social circle, then why were you so gung ho over this marriage to begin with?"

"Well, first, she's Jewish, right?"

"Essie Sue, he's a rabbi. What would you expect?"

"Worse things have happened, Ruby. Don't ask."

"So that's it? That's your selection criterion?"

"No, I also realize that the rabbi is, well, eligible but not exactly what the average Jewish girl might go for. When you add to that the fact that in general this is not the life every well-to-do Texas father would be thrilled for his daughter to get into, then . . ."

It's not often that this woman is at a loss for words.

"What you're saying is that the pickings don't look that good, huh?"

"Right."

"Okay, I'll buy that in Kevin's case, although I don't think you should rule out the fact that some people might actually consider marrying a rabbi a positive thing. You were raving about this man only months ago."

"I still think he was a wonderful end product of our somewhat limited choice, Ruby. And he has my unqualified support."

"Uh-huh. But let me point out that when you jumped on this engagement bandwagon of Kevin's, you didn't know a thing about Angel, and you still don't."

"Don't go there, Ruby. I'm sure she'll be fine. She seems to want him, and more important, the thing you haven't brought up at all is that every rabbi needs a wife. Bachelor rabbis won't cut it."

"He came here single."

"His wife left him *after* he signed our contract, remember? I'm looking out for the man's long-term career. Do you want one of our big movers and shakers trying to foist off a daughter on him, and when he doesn't date her, he loses her family's support?"

Obviously, I'm over my head here—she's given a lot more thought to this than I have. Or ever want to.

She gets back to business.

"What will you take to try on this bridesmaid's dress?"

"Nothing."

"Then let's look for another one."

She finally moves from the doorway and heads into the main part of the bridal department, where at least four "salespeople" are performing their usual duties. Selling, maybe? No. Assisting customers with questions? Definitely no. Heads down, the clerks are putting away stock—shoving even more dresses into huge racks that serve admirably to hide the sales staff from the buying public.

Hearing is not a virtue in this profession. Not even Essie Sue's less than dulcet tones can swerve them from their appointed tasks. I try to make a run for it while she's taking the telephone out of the hands of the cashier, who's been in earnest conversation with her boyfriend ever since I walked in and interrupted her a half hour ago.

Even though Essie Sue reaches out her long-taloned fingers and snags me, I have to admit that I'm on her side here. If she can get even one person to quit doing what the management obviously pays her for—marking tags and pushing racks—she'll have my vote.

She's frustrated when the cashier won't leave her post by the phone, but not for long.

"I have a strategy, when all else fails," she says.

Uh-oh—they don't know what they're in for.

Signaling me to follow her, she saunters over to the EMPLOYEES ONLY door and bursts in. Three staff members are having a coffee klatch, and are not amused when she tags the one whose pin says HI, I'M ELLEN.

"This is against the rules," two of them yell in unison,

while Ellen dashes for the exit. She's a good sprinter, but not good enough. When she actually finds herself out on the sales floor, she simply tells us, "I'm in lamps."

"Good enough," Essie Sue says.

Believe me, her expertise in lamps isn't wasted. The three-piece pink dress with matching hat they finally make me try on has me looking like one of those floor lamps with branches—the branches being stringy lace dolman sleeves with fringes that drip from elbow to wrist like pulled bubble gum strands. And that's just the jacket. The shiny shell under the open jacket is satin, and the fringes are echoed down below—the skirt is covered with them. The color is Pepto-Bismol, and my hat, if it *could* be likened to a lampshade, would pass for one only in a bordello.

"It'll do." Essie Sue ruffles up the strands and stands back, preparing, I imagine, to lie like the trouper she is.

"I'm buying," she adds, as if I'd spend a nickel of my money in this place. Ellen, our salesperson, chews her real-life bubble gum with vacant eyes and searches in vain for a getaway, since Essie Sue is standing in front of the fitting room door again. It's real comfortable in there with the three of us.

"Okay," I say, "I fulfilled my part of the bargain. I tried the thing on. I told you one dress, and that's it."

"It's your fault, Ruby. If you were bridesmaid size, you'd have a better selection."

I'm a solid size fourteen, placing me outside the pale, I guess.

Just as I'm about to be insulted, I realize I can use this. "Yep, I'm just not bridesmaid size."

"I like it anyway," Essie Sue says, changing the subject. No fool she.

I have a brainstorm. "It won't go with salmon."

"So there's more than one fish in the sea. Enough already, Ruby."

Ardis will turn purple when she sees what Essie Sue is doing to her color coordination, whoever ends up wearing this dress.

"What do you think of the dress, Ellen?" I say in a last attempt to garner support for my side. She pops her gum and seems about to offer an opinion when Essie Sue glares at her. Ellen shrugs.

"What do I know? I'm in lamps."

# 39

I'm barely home from the fitting-room fiasco when I get a call from Paul Lundy at the police station. He wants to talk about the Bogardis investigation.

"Paul, I'm so beat I can hardly stand up—it's just been one of those days."

"What's up?"

"Trust me—you wouldn't want to know."

How could I even begin to tell him that in the trunk of Essie Sue's car lies the ugliest "formal wear" Brodman's Department Store ever unloaded on an all-too-willing sucker—and it wasn't even on sale? When Ellen asked if

Essie Sue wanted to put it on layaway, I broke up—I don't even think she knows what layaway is.

"Why don't you come over here, Paul? I can offer you a blender margarita if you're willing to pretend you're off duty. Hell, you should be off duty—it's after five."

"Yeah, as if the working day ever meant anything around here."

I tell Oy Vay Paul's on his way, and throw some ice cubes, frozen limeade, Triple Sec, and tequila in the blender. Only the fanciest in this house. I have nothing else to serve him—I forgot to go to the grocery store. One of the joys of living alone is being able to exist on tuna fish and Cup-a-Soup if you can't face shopping—at least until the supplies run out and you're down to Brillo pads.

I'm in shorts, barefoot, and on my deck when Paul arrives. The three of us prepare to watch the sun go down in perfect comfort—Paul and I are stretched out on the chaise longues and Oy Vay's just stretched out. The scene would be idyllic except for the fact we're talking about murder, attempted murder, possible murder, and hard time.

"You're kidding me. Angel served time?"

"Six months when she was in her twenties," he says. "Under the name of Angel Bogardis. You were right, she and Bogie were married—the records show they were married in El Paso in 1989, and divorced in 1992. She'd had a couple of shoplifting incidents, and then took money from a spiritual publishing house where she was doing secretarial work—some scheme where she opened the checks from the mail and cashed them, and then supposedly wiped out any evidence that book orders had come in. Since she opened all the mail, she could also diddle around with the mail-order customers, tell them the shipments had been sent, and pretend to trace the packages. When she was caught, she swore she'd never seen the orders, but of course, she'd cashed the checks. I think she figured she'd be out of there by the time anyone suspected."

"So where did Bogie come in?"

"Angel said he'd thought up the whole scheme and put her up to it, but he kept his hands clean, and there was no evidence linking him to the checks. It was her place of business, her opportunity—so he was clear."

"We have to tell Kevin," I say.

"Let me handle it. I'll figure out some way to warn him. She doesn't realize we know yet, about the marriage."

"Yes, she does." I tell Paul about my conversation with Angel. "She hasn't even told Kevin she was married."

"Yeah, but now that she knows we're aware of the marriage, she'll figure out it's only a matter of time until we trace her record."

"And what about those pills? Do you think she was trying to kill him, Paul?"

"I can't think of any reason she'd want to—they aren't married yet so there's no insurance involved. Unless she thought Bogie told Kevin a lot more than he should have."

"She told me she was just trying to help Kevin lose weight, and that if the Fit and Rural people found out, she'd be in trouble."

I offer Paul another frozen margarita from the blender, but he turns it down. "I can cheat on one drink," he says, "but no more. Although I have to admit that I could use one after hearing about your conversation with Angel."

Well, I'm not on duty and I definitely want another drink.

"I'm really sorry I went so far, Paul, but when you told me I could bring up some of this with Angel, neither of us had any idea about her record."

"I'm not blaming you, Ruby, I'm just trying to decide where to go from here."

"What do you think the story is with these vitamin pills? Why is she so afraid of her bosses finding out?"

"Maybe she's giving away company property again, Ruby. She doesn't want to lose her job by having them find out she's passing out their pills to her boyfriend. You said they seem to like her there."

"Yeah, I think they do. But who knows? I certainly haven't talked to them about it—they all stay away from me after that massage that ended up in the cold room. Did you find out more about the heart attack victim, Peter Dolby?"

"That's a dead end. We have no proof of foul play, and in my opinion, at the very most those pills could have aggravated an already lethal condition. He had a bad heart before he went there."

"But my bet is the pills are being hidden as 'supplies' somewhere along the paper trail, Paul. Why would the Poundburns do that?"

"I'm sure Angel knows. On the other hand, Ruby, she

might be giving out the pills, but not be privy to anything more. I'll bet she's not the only staff member giving them out."

"You sound as if you don't think she's a player, Paul."

"I'm not sure she is. She just has a small-time feel about her. But I agree with you she's all we've got. And I'm certainly interested in the fact that Bogardis might have been blackmailing her—she has motive."

"I can't let Kevin get into this marriage not knowing about her. So what do we do?"

We don't have to ponder for more than a minute. In a word, the mountain comes to us.

My doorbell rings in an insistent fashion that can only mean Kevin's or Essie Sue's finger is on the button. It's Kevin, squeezed into a pair of royal blue bicycle pants, topped with an orange-striped rugby shirt.

"Ruby, I have to talk to you."

"Did you bicycle over?" I ask. "You look terrible."

"Bicycle? You're kidding, right?" This from the great athlete.

"No, I wasn't kidding, actually," I say. "You look as if you're out of breath."

"I'm just upset."

"Come on in. But I have to tell you that Paul Lundy is here from the police department."

He hesitates, but plunges across the doorstep anyway.

I guess I'd better throw in some more ice cubes. Paul will be staying, Oy Vay's very interested, and Kevin can use a drink. As for myself, I quickly decide two margaritas are enough. I want to be up for this.

I lead Kevin to the deck in back, and he throws himself into my chaise longue, barely glancing at Paul.

"What's happened, Rabbi?" Paul gets up from his lounger, pulls over a chair, and sits in front of Kevin. I pour Kevin a drink from our iced pitcher. He takes a big gulp and leans back—it seems to relax him.

"I don't know where to start," he says.

Paul and I both speak at once, but Paul gives me a look that says *back off,* so I keep my mouth shut. After all, he's better at this than I am. Maybe.

"Take your time, Rabbi. We're not going anywhere."

So far, so good. I guess he does have a nice touch.

"My fiancée came over to the apartment this morning," he tells Paul. "She told me some rather upsetting things, but since she says they're a matter of record and you probably know about them, I guess it's no secret. Not anymore."

Paul nods for him to go on, so he does.

"Angel made breakfast for me this morning—scrambled fake eggs just like I've learned to like them, those great soy sausages baked in the microwave, rice cakes topped with sugarless maple syrup, and Postum."

"Uh, maybe you could concentrate on what she told you," Paul says.

"Oh, yeah, well, we sat down on my bed—there's not much room in my living area—and she laid her head in my lap and told me about falling in love with Bogie. My friend Bogie—I couldn't believe it. She said she was very young and impressionable and she never should have listened to him. They were living in El Paso, and he was all revved up about being Mr. Texas Muscle.

"Bogie thought he'd be famous and be paid by all kinds of national magazines for layouts, but he found out that being Mr. Texas Muscle didn't pay a lot—it was kind of a hobby. He was hoping for a baseball career, but that's a slow process. They didn't have any money to do anything or have fun, and he thought of this scheme where she could make extra money at the place she worked. Do you want to know about how they did it?"

"We pretty much know about that from the police reports," Paul says. "We know she went to prison."

"Prison kind of broke them up," Kevin says. "They got divorced after a few years, and she asked me if Bogie had told me about the divorce in confidence during the time I knew him. I said of course he hadn't. Angel and I didn't even meet each other until after Bogie was killed. But I couldn't understand why *she* didn't tell me, the way I had told her about my divorce. She said she couldn't tell me because she was afraid it would come out that because of Bogie, she had gone to prison."

Paul asks a few questions, but nothing emerges that we don't know already. It seems that clever little Angel has pulled the sting by going to Kevin and confessing before he could find out from anyone else.

"She also told me you think she's done something very wrong by giving me those vitamin pills, and that you might tell on her to her bosses."

I start to say that our *telling on her* is the least of her worries at this point, but I keep quiet.

"I don't have to make some kind of statement about this at the police station, do I?" he asks Paul.

"Not at this point, Rabbi."

"I just can't believe she deceived me about all this. I'm the one she should have confided in. I believe at one point, she actually told me she'd never been married, so she lied to me, too. I just can't quit thinking about it. You see how shaken I am. And when I think about the wedding and the . . ."

"Oh, please, Kevin, the wedding is not something you should be worrying about right now. Essie Sue and I will take care of everything—we'll get in touch with people for you, and they'll understand."

"Understand what?"

"That—well, that you . . ."

We're staring at each other when it dawns on me that, once again, we're not on the same wavelength.

He looks at me as if I'm dummy of the month.

"Ruby, I only meant that I don't know how I can look fit and happy at my wedding next week when I've just had this shock. Angel's put me through a lot."

"Yeah. And?" I'm still incredulous.

"And what?"

"And you're still going through with it?"

"Of course, I'm going though with it. She told me she's still in love. You're not still wanting me for yourself, are you?"

Paul holds his glass out for another pour. There's just enough for the two of us.

"Where's mine? I'm the one who needs it," Kevin says.

"You need something," is all I can muster.

Damn. Just when I thought I'd escaped the specter of that putrid Pepto-pink dress.

# 40

"You're wearing black?"

Essie Sue looks me up and down with the special scorn reserved for those beyond the pale.

"You're lucky I'm here at the Temple at all, Essie Sue. If you and Kevin are nuts enough to go through with this so-called match after everything we know already, I think someone ought to wear the color of mourning—and it might as well be me." Especially if it gets me out of parading down the aisle in the Dress of the Damned.

"*Pardonez-moi,* but who's nuts? One of the things women absorb with their mother's milk is that black is not a bridesmaid's color, Ruby. You'll disgrace the wedding. We only have a couple of hours before it starts—go change." I ignore her. The dress is safely locked in her trunk, and that's where it's going to stay.

Kevin insisted on letting Essie Sue in on the secret life of Angel Elkin, aka Bogardis. As she tells it, with the rabbi on one side and Angel on the other, each asking for her blessing, how could she refuse? Paul and I are both sure she received an abbreviated and sanitized version, but the bottom line is, the bride and groom won her over. Kevin's convinced it's because she's forgiving of someone who's paid her debt to society, but I know better—she can't bear to cancel an event she's paid so much for and planned so carefully. And as far as debts to society go, I'm not sure the ledger is all that clear yet between Angel and the Universe.

"I'm going with the flow," Essie Sue tells me as we look over the decorated sanctuary of the Temple. When I say *decorated,* I don't just mean gardenia sprays dotting the aisles—I mean *decorated*. As in *tchotchkies* ad infinitum. On the bride's side of the aisle, you have your Styrofoam female angels wearing Star of David crowns, and on the groom's side, you have your Styrofoam male angels draped in Saran Wrap see-through togas. Signifying what, you might ask? As Shakespeare would say, should he be so unlucky as to be in attendance—signifying nothing.

Ardis has used the salmon theme to exhaustion—the real things are probably swimming upstream in droves to leave the territory. The ushers, who, by the way, outnumber the bridal party by ten to one, are wearing salmon-colored armbands to match their dyed handkerchiefs. The entire High Holy Days usher corps has been drafted for the occasion.

Essie Sue and Ardis are both outfitted in slinky sequined gowns—Ardis in salmon and Essie Sue in beige. I shudder to think that they coordinated this, but they probably did.

Ardis is darting between the social hall, the kitchen, and the patio. On the reception tables, the salmon-colored napkins have been radiated outward into fanlike curves, and will coordinate with the lox spread that has leapt the hurdle of the too-Jewish barrier solely because of hue.

I haven't been privy to what the bride will be wearing. I understand there's been more friction in that department between Angel and Ardis. One of the Austin rabbis will perform the ceremony, which, as Angel insists, will be "creative, not traditional." This means speechifying by the bride and groom, I suppose—promising back and forth, question and answer, and sharing. Lots of sharing.

"Let's go," Essie Sue says, jerking my arm.

"I told you I'm not changing clothes," I say.

"Not that—I gave up on that. It's dark now. I want you to sneak away with me and go for a ride."

Uh-oh—ever since I first met this woman, I've been afraid of that fateful day when she'd have me *taken for a ride*.

"Nothing doing."

"Don't fool around, Ruby—this is serious. I have a special surprise for the bride and groom that not even Ardis knows about. I'm letting you in on it, so come on."

"It must be something so heavy you can't lift it yourself," I say from experience.

"We're going back to my Center for Bodily Movement to pick it up, and we don't have all that much time to get back and forth."

She's really jerking me now, and we're halfway to the parking lot before I can get my balance.

She pushes me into the Lincoln and roars off. "Hey, I haven't even buckled my seat belt," I say.

"It doesn't matter. I'm in a hurry."

"Thanks for the concern."

"We closed early tonight, so that all the employees could attend the wedding. They've all worked out with the rabbi at various times, and have gotten to know him."

"Worked what out with the rabbi?"

"They're his exercise partners, and unlike you, they're all very happy and excited for him."

"Essie Sue, how can you be excited? You have no idea what he might be getting himself into, and neither does he."

"The lady doth protest too much, Ruby."

"You don't see disaster here? It's not the jail time—it's all the lying she's done with him."

"No, I think Angel will try harder than ever to be a wonderful rabbi's wife, and that's all that's really important to the congregation. And most important, we're all sworn to secrecy about her being in prison."

I give up, but she keeps at it.

"There's only you, the police, me, and the bride and groom. No one will ever know. This will be the event of the year, Ruby."

I sulk in my car seat for the rest of the way to the Center. Essie Sue drums her purple fingernails on the steering wheel—I can tell she's stressed out over this, even though she'd burn in hell before she'd admit it to me.

We pull up into the lot in the back of the building, and park next to the back door.

"Okay, I'm ready to tell you now," she says.

"Tell me what?"

"What we're here for, of course."

"Oh, that. Well—give."

Her face brightens, despite our glum exchanges on the way over here.

"This is really stunning, Ruby. Ardis will be green that she wasn't in on it. I think it's going to be the hit of the reception."

"Well, Ardis will be green as long as it coordinates, but tell me, already."

"I've ordered a huge ice sculpture in the likenesses of the bride and groom. They're depicted as angels hovering over the state of Israel. It's fabulous—you have to see it to believe it, Ruby."

That, I'm sure of, and I don't know that I'll believe it even *after* I see it.

"In other words, Essie Sue, it *is* heavy—right? And you need me to help get it into your car?"

"I thought you'd be privileged to do it. I didn't want anyone else entrusted with the secret."

"Flattery aside, can I ask a simple question? Why didn't you have this delivered to the Temple, which is, after all, where the wedding reception will be?"

"Because of the rabbi, of course. Sometimes you can't seem to put two and two together, Ruby. The rabbi goes to the refrigerator all the time at the Temple, and even if he didn't, someone else could see it there and tell him."

"If it were all tightly wrapped, you really think he'd even be interested?"

"Maybe not, but Ardis would."

"Oh, the light dawns. You wanted to be one up on Ardis."

"She's very efficient and I think she's earned her fee, Ruby, but just between you and me, I think she's something of a prima donna. I just want to show her what happens when you combine creativity with elegance."

"Let's see it, then. I want to know what happens, too."

We head to the kitchen entrance, and Essie Sue takes out her big set of keys. The dark kitchen is a little creepy as we open the door, but she flips the light on.

Inside the aluminum freezer is something wrapped in newspaper that looks like a forty-pound turkey—not that I've ever seen a forty-pound turkey. And I'll bet that ice that size weighs a lot more.

"Looks even heavier than I thought it would," I say.

"Can't you ever think of anything besides yourself, Ruby?"

"Yeah, I'm thinking specifically about my back."

Before I can stop her, she rips the paper off to reveal the angelic couple in all their frozen glory.

"The pièce de résistance!"

The angels over Israel don't resemble anyone I know or care to know, but I try to mute my reactions—she's clearly thrilled.

"What do you think?"

"Uh—very nice. Must have cost plenty."

"Does it look expensive?"

I guess I've touched the right button. "Oh, yeah, definitely."

"Well, it was. But they're worth it. Do you think Ardis will be impressed?"

No, but I'm not touching that one.

"How do you propose we get it out of here, Essie Sue?"

"Just good old elbow grease."

I realize it's useless to argue. We prop back the kitchen door with a wooden wedge and open the rear door of the Lincoln.

"I think you need to rewrap this," I say.

"Let's just throw some big towels over it."

"Okay, but it'll drip all over the car."

"Quit being negative, Ruby—I'll use the air-conditioning. Let's lift."

We lift. It's the heaviest thing I ever want to carry, but we make it the few feet to the car and dump it onto the backseat. I think Israel lost the Gaza Strip in the process, but who's counting?

"I think you'd better drive fast, Essie Sue—and save some of those loose ice chips for my back."

Thank goodness I refused to wear the fringed bubble gum getup—I can just picture me tripping all over myself.

I'm watching as we back out of the parking lot to make sure Essie Sue doesn't ram into anything, when I see a familiar van pulling into the back lot—or at least, almost pulling in. It stops, makes an abrupt about-face, and crunches the dust behind it in a successful attempt to race back where it came from—wherever that was.

"Who in the world was that?" Twisting around to get a better look out the back window gives me a sharp pain in neck—an apt metaphor for what the rest of the evening is going to be, I imagine. Not to mention that my lower back is already killing me.

"Just someone turning around," Essie Sue says. She's already maneuvered to the street and is putting the pedal to metal, as they say.

"Not too fast," I yell. "If you have to make a stop, you'll separate the angels before they even have a chance to mate."

"Don't be vulgar, Ruby. The clergy is involved here."

"They're involved, all right. That's what I'm worried about."

The depressing thought suddenly pops into my head that Angel might have roped Kevin into something distinctly unkosher with those pills, and I'm not just thinking bacon ramaki. Common sense is not this man's strong point, and he'd definitely be vulnerable to a smart cookie who says she loves him. I'm just not sure Angel *is* a smart cookie. But I'm still appalled that he's insisting on marrying her after all this.

"*That's* where I saw that van." The depressing thoughts are apparently ganging up on me.

"What are you talking about, Ruby?"

"That's the Fit and Rural van—I'm sure of it."

"It turned around too fast—how could you see anything?"

"I couldn't see exactly, but I'm telling you, I know that van. Why would it be here?"

"It wouldn't be. The Center for Bodily Movement is

closed, and we've announced the early closing for a week—it was in our bulletin, too."

"Maybe they're bringing over more matzo balls they've packaged—ready for the airfreight."

"Don't be silly. They do that during the day. They just brought a new shipment over this morning—I saw it myself. I could have shown it to you if we'd looked in the other freezer. It wasn't their van, Ruby."

"Okay. Mine is not to reason why at this point. I've got enough on my mind getting through the night. Aren't you nervous?"

"No. Our beloved rabbi is tying the knot, and it'll be a joyous event. This ice sculpture will be the hit of the party—just wait."

She's obsessed with the ice angels. I wish I were blessed with the ability to glorify the trivial—this wedding is one event I'd like to block out of my consciousness. In more ways than one.

Now I'm anxious to get to the Temple and unload this frozen ton of tastelessness. I suddenly have other things on my mind. As we reach the temple parking lot, I see two hefty waiters, undoubtedly hired for the wedding reception.

"Hey, guys, how about giving us a hand with this centerpiece?"

I don't dare say what kind of centerpiece—they'll find out soon enough.

Essie Sue's not pleased. "No, we should do it, Ruby. I don't trust anyone else."

"Are you kidding? We're lucky to grab these men

before they disappear. You don't want your masterpiece to melt, do you?"

I'm already waving them over, and I run to the kitchen entrance and hold the door open. Essie Sue has no choice but to open the back door of the Lincoln.

As the waiters lug the almost fallen angels across the threshold, I follow them inside and close the door behind me while Essie Sue is still locking her car—maybe this way I can escape any further calls to duty. I'm ready to head for my own car, which is fortunately parked in the front lot, so I give one call to the waiters.

"The other lady will show you where to put it—just lay it on the counter for now."

She'll *plotz* when she realizes I'm gone, but I still have an hour and a half before the wedding starts, and I'm not wasting a minute of it. I jump in my car, drive for about a block so I'm well out of Essie Sue's orbit, and pull over to the curb. It's only been about fifteen minutes total since we saw the van at the Center. I pick up my cell phone and put in a call to Paul Lundy at home.

"Yeah," he says when he realizes it's me, "I'm coming to the wedding, Ruby. Against my best interests, but I'm coming. I figure I can finish this quarter of the game before I have to get dressed."

"No, you have to leave now—forget getting dressed—just grab a jacket for later. No one was supposed to be at the Center tonight—all the staff members are invited to the wedding. But I was just out there and I saw the van from Fit and Rural—they turned and sped down the street when they saw someone was watching. I think they'll come back."

"What the hell are you talking about?"

I have to explain the whole megillah to him in detail, wasting yet more time, before he gets it.

"Okay, I'll call some uniforms on the way, and have them come with me to check the place out. See you at the wedding later. Unless I have to miss it."

"You wish. See you at the Center in ten minutes."

"Nothing doing," he says, but I've already hung up the phone, so of course I wasn't able to hear that instruction.

# 41

As I go toward the Center, I drive around the block so I can approach from the front—now the building stands between my car and anyone parked in the back lot. Contrary to what Paul thinks, I'm not brazen enough to make myself a sitting duck. I park across the street from the Center's entrance, in a pizza lot where I can still get a good view while I wait.

I can see absolutely nothing, of course, but hopefully I can creep around the corner once Paul gets here. Come to think of it, the better plan might be to wait until he's gone into the Center before I make an appearance. That way, he'll be too busy to tell me to leave.

He drives up in his own car, and circles around the back. As soon as he disappears from my sight, I move the car to the side entrance, where I have an oblique view of the back lot. Yep, the van is there—pulled up to the back door with the rear hatch open. Paul parks in the alley abutting the parking area, well away from the van. I don't see anyone sitting in the van—whoever it is must be inside already.

I'm wondering why Paul doesn't get out of the car—he seems to be watching like I am. I guess he's waiting for backup. Harmon Poundburn and that weird bear of a man who looks like a butcher come out of the Center kitchen all of a sudden—I think they've been unloading cartons from the van through the back door. The other man's name is Bud—the guy I saw in the Fit and Rural freezer room months ago. He was wearing white then, and he is now—the same white apron, pants, and tee shirt I remember from before. I see Paul on his car phone. I'm wondering if Harmon and Bud broke in, or if they had a key.

Uh-oh—Bud is lifting a carton from the van and shouting something to Harmon, who's gone inside. I can't hear a thing, but hopefully, Paul can. Bud takes the carton inside, and Paul runs toward the back door. All three men are inside now, removing the whole scene from my view.

I hear a gunshot ring out, and at the same time, Harmon dashes out the side entrance, right in front of my car. I swerve the car so it's sideways in the narrow street, and I lean on the horn. I know he can run around the car, but maybe I've slowed him down enough to alert Paul inside.

What I forget is that he can also jump on the hood,

which he does. He's got a gun out, aimed directly at me, and no matter how much I zigzag the car, I can't drop him. When he shoots a warning shot straight through the windshield and out the rear window, I get the message.

This is the point where Steve McQueen used to gun the motor and get the hell outta there in a straight line, but I'm too scared Harmon will shoot me before he falls, if he ever does. He motions to be let in, and jumps into the backseat—gun trained on me.

"Drive."

I turn the ignition the wrong way, playing for time, and the car shudders, then stops. His gun lets me know in the back of my neck that I'd better turn the key the right way, and I do. As soon as we're on our way down the street, the backup police car practically rams into us. I honk the horn until Harmon makes me stop, but the police are on the case. They slam on their brakes, and run out.

For a minute I'm sure I'll be a hostage, but Harmon doesn't have the nerve after both front tires are shot out. Two uniformed policemen surround the car, and when they yell at Harmon to drop the gun, he lets it fall on the floor behind the driver's seat. The police jerk open both doors.

"Please get him out first," I say. "I just want him out of here."

I lean against the wheel for a few minutes while they put Harmon in the police car, giving myself the luxury of thinking about absolutely nothing. That doesn't last, though, when I remember the gunshot I heard coming from the kitchen. Where's Paul?

"There was shooting inside that building," I say. "Aren't you going to see if Lieutenant Lundy is in trouble?"

They look at each other. I think they were so busy reacting to my situation that they'd forgotten the backup call. One stays with Harmon while the other races into the Center.

I wait an interminable five minutes before Paul appears just outside the door and waves at me.

"I'm fine," he says. "You okay?"

I give him a thumbs-up sign, since I'm not sure my shouting voice is working yet.

In another minute an ambulance rolls up. The attendants go inside and carry out Bud, who seems to be wounded in the right arm.

"Lady, do you need to go to be checked out, too?" The policeman watching Harmon calls out to me.

"Oh no. I'm fine." And even if I weren't, I wouldn't ride to the hospital with Bud the butcher.

Paul seems to understand I need to stay put for a while. He comes over and gets into the front seat with me.

"How's it going?"

"I'm okay—honest."

He looks at me. "You not only came here when I told you to stay at the Temple, but you took a helluva chance by taking on Poundburn."

"I was just trying to stop him from running away. I knew your backup crew hadn't come yet. At least you have him now. And Bud—looks like you did a good job subduing him."

"You're not diverting me with flattery, are you? Forget it, Ruby."

"Okay, I'm sorry. But you were in there a long time with Bud. I was worried."

"Not to worry. I got an awful lot out of Mr. Bud, I assure you."

"At least my call for you to come over wasn't a total loss."

"Not a total loss. By the way, are you up for going to that wedding, or do you want to use this for an excuse?"

The wedding? I'd forgotten all about that. I look at my watch—the wedding's scheduled to start in forty-five minutes.

"Of course I don't want to go. But why is it even on your mind, Paul? You're not exactly a fan of Kevin's."

"Get out of the car a minute, Ruby. I want to see what shape you're in. The uniforms filled me in on the gun to your back. I want to see for myself."

We both get out, and he makes me walk around on my own.

"See? I told you I was fine. I'm not passing out. At least, not until I get home with Oy Vay later tonight. In fact, I'm energized. The letdown usually comes later."

"Just making sure. If you're up for it, I wanted you to let me escort you to that wedding."

"If this is a date, I'll eat that badge in your pocket, Lundy. What's cooking?"

He looks at me, and we both laugh. Too bad we're destined to be such good friends.

"What's cooking is that I need to be at that wedding, and my going alone—with you not there at all, could attract more attention than I'd like. I was only asked as a friend of yours, anyway."

"That's where you're wrong, Paul—they've invited most of Eternal."

"Well, whatever the deal is, if I can extract a promise from you to stay on the sidelines, you might get to see the other half of today's little drama."

"Whoa—that's tempting. And don't worry about my staying on the sidelines—I don't have the energy to do anything else."

"And I want you to promise you won't say anything about what's happened here to anyone—especially not to Essie Sue."

"But she's bound to be called anytime, right? I'm sure there's plenty of damage in the kitchen."

"I've got investigators on their way—this is a crime scene now. And yes, you're right that this news won't keep long, but I'm betting on some time while everyone's concentrating on the wedding. And we have Harmon and Bud en route for the moment."

"You're the boss."

"We'll leave your car for the tow truck, in case you were concerned."

"*Oy,* my car. How am I going to get around next week?"

"That's the least of your worries right now. Let's get in my car, stop at a service station for a quick cleanup, and I'll get you to the church on time. Jewish style, of course."

"You're awfully high, Lundy, for someone who was just in a gunfight."

"Let's just say I'm hopeful."

"Tell me something—what exactly were Harmon and Bud doing in the gym kitchen?"

"I was wondering when you were going to recover from the shock of that ride and start asking questions. Jump in the car and I'll fill you in on the way."

# 42

We check in at the Temple with a half hour to spare. A few of the older people have arrived early, but the place is basically empty. I take Paul around to one of the classrooms they're using as a bridal dressing room—just so everyone will know we're here. As I guessed, this part of the joint is jumping—it's headquarters for everyone from Essie Sue and Ardis to the nervous bride and groom.

I'm so distracted from my adventure at the Center I forget that Essie Sue's probably furious with me for running off and leaving her with the ice sculpture. She glares at me.

"I thought you'd at least have a good excuse," she says,

"like surprising me by going home and changing into your bridesmaid dress."

"I couldn't. It's still in the trunk of your car. And trust me, you wouldn't have wanted me in it on this particular day."

"When else?"

"Never mind—what's that you're giving Angel?" Any distraction in a storm.

"It's what she's *trying* to give me," Angel says. "It's supposed to be something old, something new, something borrowed, something blue. She's trying to give me turquoise."

Essie Sue holds up a faux turquoise pin in the shape of a Star of David.

"I just borrowed it from the temple gift shop," Essie Sue says. "It's made in Israel, so how can she say it's not appropriate? It can serve as something borrowed *and* something blue."

Ardis jerks the pin out of Essie Sue's hand. "You're upsetting my bride, in case you haven't noticed. It's unlucky not to give blue. And turquoise is definitely not blue. Got it?"

"Looks like things are getting out of hand here," Paul whispers to me.

"Boys *out*," Ardis orders, pointing to Paul. "You and the rabbi leave. Angel has to get dressed."

"Do you want me to save you a seat?" Paul says.

"No, I have to stand up as the bridesmaid, remember?"

Ardis pushes him out the door with Kevin, and closes it. "So, Ruby, why don't you find Angel something blue?"

"I'm sure Essie Sue can handle the challenge," I say.

"I'm having nothing more to do with it," Essie Sue says. "I provided the old and the new, and that's the end of it. The *old* is a piece of wedding cake from my very own wedding."

Yuck. I wonder where she tucked *that*. Hope Angel doesn't nibble it by mistake.

"The *new,*" Essie Sue adds, "is the invoice Ardis just gave me from Weddings Anonymous. Just so Angel knows where all this is coming from."

This is what happens when you lie down with the likes of whomever.

Ardis isn't satisfied. "Essie Sue, I'm losing patience. This is Angel's day. Humor her by getting something borrowed and blue. Quick."

"She can borrow my fountain pen," I joke. "It has blue ink."

"It'll do," Ardis says.

"But I was kidding."

I guess you don't kid around these two. Ardis holds her hand out until I fumble in my purse for the pen. I'm surprised they don't ask to test the ink.

"She's all fixed up for luck now," Ardis informs us, "so let's get her dressed."

"I'll be back in a minute," Essie Sue says. "You get started."

Angel is wearing white. Yards and yards and yards of white tulle, coordinated with salmon trim, leaving her listing leeward as she tries to walk and keep her train straight. With her previous husband Bogie's murder not yet solved, the purity routine rings a bit false to me, but I guess I'm prejudiced.

Ardis is ecstatic. "An Ardis Sommerfield creation," she says when we get Angel decked out. "As is the whole upcoming production."

Before I can get too nauseous, Essie Sue comes back in with a suspiciously familiar plastic garment bag.

"Ardis and I wanted to make one last appeal, Ruby. Please don't ruin this wedding by wearing mourning clothes." She tears open the bag and reveals the Pepto-Bismol special in all its fringed glory.

"Nothing doing," I say, as both women, assisted by Angel, start taking off my black dress. Within seconds I'm done up in the bridesmaid's special. After almost being taken hostage by Harmon Poundburn tonight, I don't have the strength to ward off this second hostage attempt. And I'm too interested in Paul Lundy's timetable to care about putting up a real fight.

Ardis takes Angel's arm and leads her to meet her groom. Essie Sue grabs *my* arm—but only to make sure I don't escape. This is a coordinated effort—and I don't just mean the white and the salmon colors.

# 43

Our bridal party is assembled in the large foyer leading into the temple sanctuary. I'm peeking through the big oak doors to see where Paul is seated. He's on the groom's side—toward the back, of course—I know he considers himself an observer, not a participant.

The Fit and Rural crowd are closer to the front, on the bride's side. I see the PR guy Sonny with Hetty Poundburn, who's looking at the door—if she's wondering where her hubby, Harmon, is, she'll have a long wait. Although it's more likely that he planned to skip the wedding and make his run out to the Center for Bodily Movement while everyone else was preoccupied with the ceremony. It seems like days—not just hours—since the police grabbed Harmon out of my car.

Minna Hoffman has just finished singing "Habanera" from *Carmen*.

"It's a surprise," Essie Sue tells us. "I thought it would bring a touch of class to the occasion."

"But Carmen was a slut," Angel says. "And she smokes. You know how opposed I am to cigarettes."

"It's in French, Angel," Essie Sue says. "Ergo, class. And it's familiar to everyone—did you hear how they were humming along?"

Ardis rolls her eyes as she smoothes out Angel's veil. "Out of line for a wedding, entirely. I told you to use 'You'll Never Walk Alone.' You wouldn't have had a dry eye in the house."

Essie Sue ignores her, and props the door open a crack with one of the corsage boxes. "The rabbi looks elegant in his tie and tails. But why does he have on those thick black boots?"

"So he'll be sure to crush the glass when he steps on it," Angel says.

"He's beaming at the congregation. Look, Angel."

"I'm not supposed to see him before the wedding."

"He's not supposed to see *you*. It doesn't work both ways—and besides, he's already been in the dressing room." I can't believe I'm having to explain this. "You take over for me, Ardis—that's what you're getting paid for."

"Take over what? You haven't done anything helpful since you've been here."

"What happened to *Fiddler on the Roof*?" I say, desperately trying to keep Essie Sue and Ardis apart.

"It's next," Essie Sue says. "'Sunrise, Sunset.' It's become like the second national anthem for our people."

"And *The Sound of Music*?"

"We nixed it in our last meeting," Essie Sue says.

"Especially since the bride and groom's favorite song from it was 'Do-Re-Mi,'" Ardis adds. "Go figure how we'd work in *'D* for female deer,' or whatever the line is."

"I still love it," Angel says. "It's a tribute to the animals and could have been very politically savvy at the same time."

They have Angel lined up at the door, with me in front of her—my face as pink as my outfit—as we hear the first bars of "Sunrise, Sunset," soon to be followed by our cue—"Here Comes the Bride."

At first, I don't believe I'm hearing a phone ringing in the middle of a temple ceremony—unless Kevin is using his cell phone for special effects. Surely the rabbi hasn't conjured up yet another surprise in honor of his wedding. Then I realize the rings are coming from our side of the door—deep within the beaded silver evening bag Ardis has hanging from her shoulder. Heads are turning in the other room—I haven't heard so much buzzing from the pews since the rabbi called for silent prayer after announcing his engagement this spring. Actually, I wish I'd prayed a little more myself after that bombshell.

Ardis lets go of her protective grip on the bride's shoulder and reaches into her purse. She has the presence of mind to try to whisper *hello,* listens for a minute, and then totally loses it.

*"What?"* Ardis is yelling now.

Essie Sue quickly slams the door to the sanctuary. "Sshh!" she hisses. "People will hear."

As it turns out, this is the understatement of the year. Just when the organist launches into the first stately bars of "Here Comes the Bride" and all heads are *supposed* to turn, our bridal consultant does three things in less than thirty seconds. She drops the phone, retrieves a lady-sized silver revolver from her purse, and grabs the bride in a choke hold with one gloved hand while shoving the gun into her back with the other.

"You ratted!" Ardis screams with her back against the door. "I'm getting us out of here."

I'm too dumbfounded to absorb anything but the fact that her silver gun coordinates with her evening bag.

Angel, in a gesture that might be fast but sure is stupid, defends herself by lifting up her leg and pulling a switch-blade from one of the pair of white Birkenstocks she's rhinestoned and covered over with tulle netting. The blade slips right out of a little pocket she's fastened between two straps. The trouble is that even though her hands are free, she has nowhere to go with the knife since she can't turn away from Ardis's grip. Ardis edges the two of them toward the doors to the outside.

The ordinary facts of life don't seem to bother Angel at the moment. She jerks her arm backward and aims the knife at Ardis's thigh just behind her. The blade passes through her own gown and Ardis's dress like teeth through cotton candy. Ardis loses her grip and goes down, shooting wildly now. There's blood on the white wedding dress as Angel's knife slips from her hand and disappears into the flowing tulle.

I'm crouching on the floor, scared to death of those wild shots. Since I'm on the other side of Ardis, out of her view for the moment, all I can do to try to stop the shooting is to yank off my huge pink fringed jacket and plop it over her head like the lampshade it is.

It's hard to believe that these fireworks have probably taken less than a minute. I can hearing Paul yelling and pounding on the doors between the sanctuary and the foyer. Why doesn't he just open them and come in? I don't see him yet, but he's taken precautions—three policemen are bursting through the tall entrance doors leading out to the front steps of the building.

"Her gun—grab it!" I point to Ardis's gun lying loosely in her hand while she's trying vainly with the other hand to rip my fringed jacket off her head. Damned if those lace fringes aren't sticking to her face like wet spaghetti.

One of the cops grabs the gun from her while she's still disoriented. She sinks to the floor and now, with both hands free, finally pulls the jacket from her face and cradles her bleeding thigh in her hands. The look she gives the bride is not one I'd want to be in the same universe with, if I were Angel.

"I knew you were a lightweight the minute I met you," Ardis says, "the weak link in the chain. I'm supposed to be so clever—why was I stupid enough to let you in on this?"

"But I didn't—I didn't say anything, Ardis. You have to believe me. I never told anyone what was going on at the ranch. I didn't give you away." Angel's wedding dress is reddening under the right arm as she speaks, but she doesn't seem to notice it.

"If you were so sure you had nothing to fear from us, then why did you carry a knife to your own wedding?"

"I carry it everywhere—ever since I first found out what was going on at the ranch. And it worked—the knife threw you off-balance, didn't it? Just when you were ready to shoot."

Which reminds me. "Angel's knife fell into her tulle skirt," I tell the police. I think I'll feel safer with all the weapons confiscated.

I look to see how Essie Sue's holding up. Now I see why Paul hasn't appeared. Essie Sue has locked the doors to the sanctuary and she's standing with her back to the doors and facing all of us—she must be in deep shock. I go over to try to pry her loose.

"It's okay, Essie Sue. The shooting is over, and as you can see, the police are here. They have all the weapons. You're going to be fine."

"Fine? Are you crazy? There's a congregation in there, and they're expecting a wedding from their rabbi. Ruby, can't you take the bride's place at the last minute? It's a shame for that gorgeous reception to go to waste."

With every beige sequin in place and still unscathed, she puts her arm around the remains of my bridesmaid's dress.

"I'll make it worth your while, Ruby. I promised Angel a Mexican honeymoon. For you, I'll spring for Europe."

# 44

"You know, Ruby, if you'd be a full-time partner here at The Hot Bagel instead of trying to fix Eternal's computer messes, you'd be better off."

"Yeah, and a lot poorer. The consulting fees are my bread and butter, if you'll pardon the expression. The bagel partnership is an investment—if I hung around more, you'd have me filling in for minimum-wage workers. I can do better letting my money work for me here while I bring in some decent fees to pay my bills."

Milt and I are sitting around the big wooden table after hours—my favorite time. I can still smell the last of the bagels from the ovens, and we've pulled out our secret stash of Kenya coffee to go along with still-warm pumpernickel bagels and some very special lox. We're trying to finish off the good stuff before our invited guests arrive.

"This lox is too good for Essie Sue," Milt says.

"I don't know what you're worried about—she doesn't eat real food, anyway."

He pours us more steaming Kenya roast. "So how's the rabbi?"

"Brokenhearted, now that Angel's in jail. But you can see for yourself when he gets here. Her wounds turned out to be superficial—Ardis's bullet just grazed her."

"You think she'll be sent away for long?"

"Well, she's not a first-timer. On the other hand, she doesn't seem to have been in on Bogie's murder—just on the scheme to transport illegal shipments of that reducing drug Deduct. But she *was* being cut in on the profits—just enough, I figure, to keep her quiet."

"They don't think she killed him? But wasn't she the link to Bogie in the first place?"

"She was. He moved to Eternal when the Mr. Texas Muscle career fizzled, and got a job as a personal trainer at Essie Sue's Center for Bodily Movement. He should have left well enough alone—Essie Sue was buying him all sorts of expensive baseball equipment and giving him a lot of authority."

"Why didn't he just stick with her?"

"He got ambitious. When he heard that Angel's bosses had big plans for a celebrity fitness ranch south of here, he was hot to work at Fit and Rural, too. He threatened to expose her prison stint, and made her get him a job at the ranch on a part-time basis—without telling Essie Sue about the moonlighting, of course."

"So where did he learn about the pill operation—from Angel?"

"Nope, he learned about it all by himself."

We hear a car pull up in back—that would be Essie Sue and Kevin. Kevin's been in touch with Angel, and I'm hoping he can fill us in on some of what the police are keeping mum about during their investigation. While I'm at it, I want to grill Essie Sue on some of the details of her arrangement with Fit and Rural.

She and Kevin both look the worse for wear. I guess they deserve some of the good lox, so I sit them down and pour the Kenya, too. Essie Sue's blouse is even half untucked—this is a first.

"I've never been more humiliated in my life than trying to explain to that congregation that we weren't having a wedding," she says. "I'll never get over it."

"How about me?" Kevin wails.

"You, too," she says. "But you're not a very good judge of character."

I'm ready to pound her, but I want something from her, so I hold my tongue. This only encourages her.

"And that Ardis . . ."

"What about Ardis, Essie Sue?"

My instincts were right—she's only too happy to comply.

"Well, most of my information comes from my insurance company lawyers—the ones who are handling the property damage claims from the gunfight at my Center. They've nosed out the case from people close to the police—no thanks to your friend Lundy, Ruby. He's not talking during the investigation."

"What did they say?"

"Ardis was running the diet pill scam, along with partners from Chicago. Can you believe it? They thought the out-of-the-way location of the fitness ranch was a perfect place to serve as a distribution point for Deduct—it got banned in the U.S. last year. They were planning to import it from South America and Europe, but shipments in other locations had been intercepted several times, and they needed a better cover."

"Enter your matzo ball scheme, huh?" Milt says. "No wonder they were so happy to work with you."

Essie Sue gives him her drop-dead stare. "Look, Milt, the Temple was benefiting from those checks I got weekly from them. They showed me how the matzo balls could be a year-round money-raiser—not just at Passover. We were doing a great service sending them all over the country. And besides, you know how hard I'm trying to raise the money for the memorial statue in memory of my sister Marla. People haven't been very generous."

"Those checks Fit and Rural sent you were a drop in the bucket to them," he answers. "You thought the money was coming from all your new customers?"

"Fit and Rural were my distributors—they collected the money and sent me the checks. Wanna make something of it, Milt?"

I realize I'd better do something quick before the well runs dry.

"This is fascinating, Essie Sue. Keep going."

"Well, as you know, my volunteers cooked the matzo balls at my Center. The Fit and Rural staff picked them up and took them to their big kitchen for processing. They froze them and packed the balls into cartons for shipping. Then, during the working day, they delivered the cartons back to the Center packed in dry ice, where the express trucks would pick them up."

"Why didn't the trucks just pick them up at Fit and Rural?" Milt's nitpicking.

"I have no idea. When I asked, they just said this was the way they wanted it done."

"Sure—because they didn't want to be a part of the shipping address. This way, they could stay completely clean," I say. "So the pills were packed into certain matzo ball cartons before they were frozen?"

"My lawyers say it was foolproof," Essie Sue says. "Right into the matzo balls. No one was going to disturb those frozen shipments. The cartons they loaded in the daytime were regular matzo balls, and the ones they brought over at night, after the Center closed, contained matzo balls stuffed with drugs."

"But how did they receive the pills to begin with?" I ask.

"At first, they were shipped to the ranch along with the new fitness equipment. But later, when they were afraid of discovery, they had bogus clients from California bring in the pills in person."

"Angel's innocent," Kevin breaks in. "Or almost innocent." He's scarfing down the bagels and lox.

"Have you talked to her?" I ask. "Does she know anything about Bogie's murder?"

"Sure she does. That's why she carried a knife around those people. She's told the police everything she knows."

"So spill it, Kevin. What's the story? Did Ardis kill Bogie?"

"No, she was there, but claims she only wanted Harmon and Bud to scare Bogie. When they overreacted, though, she was the one who figured out how to cover up the murder."

"Start at the beginning and tell us everything Angel told you." I don't want to miss any of this.

"Okay." Kevin's gulping coffee now. "Angel said Bogie was working late one night at Essie Sue's Center when he saw Bud and Harmon unloading a few boxes, to be picked up by the express shippers with the other matzo ball shipments. But the regular loads were always delivered to the Center in the daytime, so Bogie starts wondering about these night deliveries. He told Angel to mention to her bosses that he knew about the midnight runs."

"Uh-oh." I see what's coming, and so does Milt.

"Uh-oh is right," Milt says to me. "That did him in."

"Don't interrupt me," Kevin says, "I'm getting to the murder part. Angel told Ardis about Bogie's discovering the matzo ball deliveries. I had also mentioned to Angel that Bogie was going to have an appointment with Ruby and me to discuss uniforms, and Angel told Ardis that, too. Ardis panicked. I guess she thought she hadn't responded fast enough to Bogie's threats. When she phoned Bogie to come out to the ranch and talk, he was evasive—maybe to keep her guessing or because he really didn't want to go out there before he had more to go on."

"I don't blame him." Milt snorts.

"Well, at any rate," Kevin says, "even though Angel begged her not to, Ardis drove Harmon and Bud to Essie Sue's Center so they could take him in the van and bring him out to the ranch. They wanted to put a good scare into Bogie that would shut him up until a payoff or a better job could be worked out with him."

"How do you know this?" I ask. "All this is coming from your talk with Angel?"

"No," Essie Sue chimes in. "That pretentious Ardis has been talking like crazy to the police—my lawyers are getting an earful from the gossip mill. She claims all she wanted to do was have her guys get him in the van. As a cover, she even brought along a couple buckets of half-processed matzo balls—if anyone saw her, she could say they were bringing them to the ranch for packing."

"I'm telling this, Essie Sue," Kevin says.

It's always been a mystery to me how Kevin can experience such mood changes when he's in oratory mode. Suddenly, he's not the pained lover, but the performer.

"Stay with me now," he tells us, warming up to his subject. "Bogie is just setting up for batting practice. Bud calls to him, he goes over to the van, sees the buckets of matzo balls, and then realizes that Harmon is there, too. Ardis doesn't know if he sees her or not. He grabs a handful of matzo balls to throw at their faces as a diversion, and tries to run toward the practice field. Bud and Harmon snatch him before he can get away."

"So how did he end up dead?" I ask.

"He's a strong guy and they're having to force him into

the back of the van," Kevin says. "Bud has his hand over Bogie's mouth, but Bogie bites him and he almost loses his grip. Before Ardis can even react, Harmon takes a hammer from the toolbox on the floor, hits him on the forehead, and he falls. The guys panic, and Ardis figures he may be dead or dying."

"Ardis," Milt says, "is the only one of those three with brains, anyway. She must have gone into overdrive."

"Yeah," Kevin says. "She has them carry him over to the batting spot and lay him on his back, with the bat near his hand and the other equipment lying around. She says it will look as if he were hit with a ball. Just as she's going to the batting machine to find a ball she can leave by the body, they hear noises. They've been lucky so far, because it was such a wet and cold night out that the backyard was deserted. Ardis tells them to scoop up the matzo balls Bogie threw, and take off."

I'm thinking of Paul finding that matzo ball in Bogie's pocket.

"So do you think maybe he was trying to tell us something when he put that in his pocket?" I ask Milt.

"You mean, like saying 'follow the matzo meal trail'? I doubt it, considering the violent nature of his death. He wouldn't have had time to think about it, unless it's true that he wasn't dead yet when they laid him out on his back. Can you stand to think there's something you might never know, Ruby?"

"Don't be snide. If they killed Bogie before he had a chance to talk to us, though, why do you think they locked us in the cold room? We wouldn't have been a threat."

"My Angel said they were just trying to frighten us," Kevin says, "in case he *had* been in touch with us."

"*Your* Angel? She knew about locking us up, and she still didn't say anything to you? This is your idea of love?" I was feeling sorry for Kevin and Angel for a minute there, but now I'm reminded of what we went through, and I'm furious all over again.

Milt pours me another cup of coffee to calm me down. "They probably weren't sure *what* you knew," he says. "The rabbi was Bogie's friend and Angel's sweetheart, and you were making a nuisance of yourself at the ranch. I'm sure they did want to put a scare into you."

"While we're at it, who were Svetlana and Husband?" I ask Kevin. He shrugs.

"I know more details than he does," Essie Sue says. Always the competitor. "They were two new employees who were willing to be bought. End of story. And they had no connections in the area, so no one had to worry about their ratting the ranch out."

I don't know which was worse—being chloroformed at the massage table or being caught at the wedding between the Two Femmes in the Foyer.

"Who called Ardis on her cell phone?" I'm trying to unclench my fists and deal with the facts rationally, but it's not working.

"Poundburn's lawyer—Harmon had called him from the police station and asked him to alert Ardis," Essie Sue answers.

"She must have thought Angel tipped the police to go to the Center," I say.

"She did think that," Kevin says. "Angel is petrified they'll come after her in jail. Ardis still doesn't believe that you and Essie Sue drove over there on your own to pick up the ice sculpture."

Just what Essie Sue needs to hear. "*Oy,* the Angels Over Israel. This was a work of art, people, and to think I had to send it over to the Goodwill."

"You did what?"

"Well, what else could I do—smash it? At least the homeless could appreciate it. Don't remind me."

"I'm sure Goodwill was thrilled to see it coming in the door."

"That's their job, Ruby. Your concern is always misplaced. What should be worrying you is this whole wedding mess—imagine if my sister Marla's memorial statue had been built and in place at the Temple—five thousand pounds of marble down the drain from a few gunshots. The whole fiasco is a *shanda* for the community. That's a disgrace for the whole town," she translates for Milt.

"I know what it means, Essie Sue. I've been through a few of your *shandas.*"

"I hope this teaches you a lesson, Rabbi."

"What lesson?" I ask.

"He should be more careful who he drags to the altar."

"Well, I'm standing by my woman," Kevin says. "I'll wait for her to get out of prison, no matter how long it takes."

Essie Sue's face is white. "Are you crazy, Rabbi?"

"This is a private matter, and my public will just have to put up with it."

Gee, where have I heard that before?

E-mail from: Nan
To: Ruby
Subject: *Tulle Madness*

I agree with Milt that you might consider staying safely ensconced at The Hot Bagel for a while, babe. Although come to think of it, that's not exactly a murder-free zone, is it?

You asked me to look up that diet drug Deduct. It's a combination of fenfluramine and phentermine, and the word is it causes valvular heart disease—about a third of people who take the combination show signs of valvular heart damage. Deduct has been withdrawn from the market, but people are still dying to get it—if you'll pardon the expression.

I'm struggling over finals, but if all goes well, you can count me as a first-year survivor! Send me good vibes, and don't forget to keep me posted on Everything.

E-mail from: Ruby
To: Nan
Subject: *The Worm Turns*

I'm crossing fingers and toes for you during exam week—I know you'll not only survive, but triumph.

Thanks for researching Deduct—I can see dress sizes all over the country swelling up from eights to sixteens now that the source has dried up! Kevin's damn lucky he didn't take the pills for a longer time.

The Fit and Rurals are falling all over themselves to be the first to make a deal. Bud started spilling information as soon as Paul caught him unloading the truck at Essie Sue's Center the night of the wedding. He told Paul about Ardis—that's why Paul had the police waiting outside the Temple. I don't think he anticipated that melee, though.

Harmon swears Ardis masterminded the whole thing, but she claims she had no intention of harming Bogie. Meanwhile, the ones who aren't worried about murder raps are still up to their necks in the illegal drug scheme.

You asked to be kept posted, and do I have an update for you!

Rabbi Kevin (stand by my woman) Kapstein has just written a letter to the congregation (with a little help from his mentor):

*My Dear Congregants,*

*It is with profound sorrow that I announce the dissolution of my engagement to Ms. Angel Elkin on the grounds of gross incompatibility. Recent events have forced me to question the fitness of Ms. Elkin to serve as the wife of your Spiritual Leader and as a Role Model to the women and children of the congregation.*

C'est la vie *with regret, as the saying goes—and we shall go forward from strength to strength.*

*I write this letter as I fly to Europe, where I am taking a two-week respite from recent aggravations.*

*Yours En Route,*
*Rabbi Kapstein*

Just think, Nan, I could've been sharing that airline seat with Kevin at this very moment, if only I hadn't let the whole wedding go to waste.

P.S. If he had to be bought, I sure hope he held out for first class!

# Ruby's Basic Matzo Ball Soup

## *Matzo Balls*

½ cup matzo meal (can be purchased in supermarkets and groceries)
1 tsp. salt
2½ tbsps. chicken fat
2 eggs
3 tbsps. soup stock

Mix matzo meal and salt, then add a mixture of chicken fat and slightly beaten eggs. Blend thoroughly and add soup stock. Cover and refrigerate for at least an hour, then form mixture into marble-sized balls or larger, wetting hands to form balls. Drop or ladle balls into boiling, salted water in a large pot. Cover pot and cook for 30–35 minutes at slow boil. Add matzo balls to freshly made chicken soup. Makes one dozen matzo balls or less, depending on size.

## *Chicken Soup*

1 large chicken, cut in pieces
Salt and pepper as desired
1 onion, peeled and quartered
3 carrots, sliced round
Several pieces of celery

Place thoroughly washed chicken in large kettle with enough water to cover all pieces—about four quarts. Boil until froth appears—then reduce boil to medium and remove froth. Add salt, pepper, onion, carrots, and celery. Cook covered until pieces of chicken are tender, at least two hours. Remove all vegetables and chicken if desired, and gently add matzo balls to soup before serving. Serves eight, depending on portions. Enjoy!

## Essie Sue's Matzo Ball Soup, with notes

*Matzo Balls*

Directions: Use ingredients as per Ruby's recipe, with the following exceptions:

2 eggs—Don't even think about it . . . you wouldn't want the cholesterol. Try egg whites.
2½ tbsps. chicken fat—Is Ruby crazy? Look what happened to the *chicken* with all that fat. Forget it.
1 tsp. salt—In your dreams. Causes high blood pressure.

Conclusion for cooks: You should be buying my diet matzo balls in the first place. Don't try to prepare them yourself. Since the ingredients are top secret, you can't make them on your own without a lawsuit pending.

## *Chicken Soup*

The onion, celery, carrots, and pepper in Ruby's recipe are okay. (The froth might be low in calories, but you never know.) As for the chicken, try swirling a chicken wing back and forth in the boiling water—that should do the trick. If not—tough. This will make you have empathy for all those years our people were in the desert.

Enjoy!

## About the Author

Sharon Kahn has worked as an arbitrator, attorney, and free-lance writer. She is a graduate of Vassar College and the University of Arizona Law School. The mother of three, and the former wife of a rabbi, she lives in Austin, Texas. Following several children's books published regionally, *Fax Me a Bagel,* the first Ruby, the Rabbi's Wife novel and Sharon Kahn's mystery debut, appeared in 1998.